CIGARETTES AROUND THE ROOM

CIGARETTES AROUND THE ROOM

Cadan Henry

BURDEN BOOKS
Indianapolis

www.cadanhenry.com

Published in the United States by
Burden Books, Indianapolis

FIRST SOFTCOVER EDITION 2010 OCTOBER

Burden ISBN 978-0-578-06034-7

BURDEN BOOKS
PO Box 501938, Indianapolis, IN 46250

PRINTED IN THE UNITED STATES OF AMERICA

For my fathers, mothers, brothers and sisters.

CIGARETTES AROUND THE ROOM

Book I

Parents' marriage dissolved years back, was ten, been living since with my father. His new situation the result of an epidemic he told me; *it's hitting everyone.* Seems as though he was right. Studying constantly under his supervision, sheltered, protected from the outside he didn't trust. He was still tolerable except for the fear. Divorce would always tear at him. He'd never fully recover. When my mother moved out of state with my younger brother so much changed. None of us ever lived apart. One is enough she told me when I asked why not take both of us? I watched my father pull back, become a different man. Hurt to see him that way, expected me too young to understand. Despite our challenges raised me in old discipline, did this alone for almost six years with faith and confidence I wasn't able to see because often I worried he had little of either. We stayed put, didn't move from town. Remember it slippery green, empty brown, river cutting through, homogenous people, affable, those pious thugs folded in. We dwelled in a smaller house, older neighborhood, purchased after a lot of inconvenience.

Had a job as a line cook. Worked long hours, usually staying as late as the boss would let me. Wasn't my first job, had others. Mowing. Shirt factory. Father advocated work; let me do it before other things. If you were willing age should not matter he believed. Kept me out of the house, money in my pocket, a new benefit I easily got used to. Working, school, good routine, sick of one, do the other. One teacher an unusually involved woman, tried watching over me, sensitive to the inconstant life I had, believe she coddled me more, got off thinking she might want me. Made myself hard to find. No shortage of reasons, avoid having to cope with dad's second wife, her four children. After so long the two of us my father finally remarried a couple years ago. Stepmother and he knew each other eight months. Kids went silent allowing them their chance. The one story house we all shared was not big enough with three bedrooms and only one bathroom. Had been for dad and me but wasn't anymore. We were too many, living on top of one another. Place constantly filled with turmoil and tension. No one clear on why they were there, resentment and bitterness from events past. I'd been moved to the basement, stepsister was in my old room.

The money I was making meant I didn't have to depend on anyone, didn't have to ask for anything, used it to go around a weird life. Bought a car almost a year ago, my birthday. They didn't want me to have it, no good reason I remember. Went to all the lots on our side of town with my stepbrother who loved cars. We found something extraordinary. A dark gray two seater. Got in, drove it, had to have it. Tore down the road, was a stick, frightened our hustler passenger. Sales guy thought we were dealing drugs to afford it and wanted in. I found bits of tobacco stuck to the fabric and in crevices. He told us the owner was a pipe smoker. Calm, easy on the vehicle. The purchase cost me everything and more.

Used to go out after work with fellow employees. Grill man, certain waitresses, couldn't imagine them working anywhere else. Got to drink beer, tried to feel each other up. Talked about ambitions, flirted, hinted at sex. When I got home just told whoever demanded I had to work late. Usually quelled their natural suspicion but sometimes the new wife wanted a fight regardless, disliked her life like me, the one that she let know.

We all feel singled out, thought she went out of her way for me. Unconscionably, a woman just as vicious as any man. I wished all the time for independence. Idea heavy on my mind. Took comfort knowing soon would be the beginning of a life was till now only a disobedient vision.

I graduated that June, friends, classmates and I attended the usual ceremony, ditched our families, drank ourselves sick under the stars. Placated our parents by telling them we were staying at a friend's house. Folks never suspected, they were happy, so was I. Thought it would have been a more memorable night, turned out to be only another day going past. Road sign along a time line. Something to go by, leave behind till enough of them had gone by then I would be there.

Emotional barriers in the house grew deep, well guarded and I was still naïve about going off alone. I'd never done it, didn't know anything about it but being stuck in the dark kept me from worrying too much. Hard to accept I might not be able to rely on them again for support of any kind. This thought came, was somewhat terrifying but I knew it was important not to correct in reverse. Everything would depend on me now. The revolution to rest under battling fury of short wings. Goo covered newborn. Though certainly unprepared, wasn't difficult to remain resolute centrally, through the solar plexus.

◆

Dad sank to false optimism. Hard to distinguish. A kind of man who would say anything meaning well but that just couldn't come true. Took a while to see till I'd lived through some of it then taught myself to look ahead and go around. Been nice to get the money when the time came, help pay for all the school. Well known university which wasn't far. He didn't look at me sadly, maybe like he was getting out from underneath.

I needed to sell the car. Had some extra money to get started, couldn't let my plans come apart. The time was too close. Afraid the joke might die.

I put the car on the market days before I was supposed to leave and my stepmother said she would handle the sale while I was away. I decided to trust her. Think she accepted I needed to go. Felt like we were all going really. I don't re-member much about the day before. The packing, good byes. Maybe I was numb, so tense nothing stuck. Already aloft for some time. Experiencing the real moment stunned me awake like I had never been as all my longing, living ahead in antic-ipation came to the lead. Numbness protecting against fear of what was unmended.

The college only about two hours off, in the same state but may as well have been across the continent. The number of times they came to visit and that I returned over the year ahead would be few. Discovered we were not at all close, did not care to be I guess. Told ourselves we'd live like that because too much had happened. Where would we begin? Even if we did face things no one could have endured it. So now we kiss off on beyond.

The details of my arrival, at the school, like the day before, elude me. Was it my Dad? My stepbrother? Who brought me, left me standing by the curb that afternoon is something I still wonder about. Excitement of getting away, living someplace new had overtaken me. A better life waited. Hope sprung; white light filled my mind in a bristly flash, in the absence of bitterness, reckoning the life I'd reclaim. Gone away at last. Didn't know what would happen now, did know I was going to be unbound, loose from a great deal. My life would be mine. Wanted it so badly. Speaking the first and last word. No more standing bouncing on top of the sofa, screaming, fighting. Yeah. But it was the feeling of guilt, mostly, that I wouldn't miss, the accompanying awful dread. The mood melted, allowed to try and know myself.

The years took their toll and we were worn down after so long slamming into one another. All of us left empty as broken glass. Many nights it was too much, split families and their propensity for violence, half the house sobbing itself to sleep. I came to realize there was part of me I didn't want to know. Foreign, disturbing and even brutal. It didn't belong. Inside, moving around, separate, rooted in anxiety and fatigue and panic. Afraid of where it came from, troubled me so much to think about, worry, usually, to solve it.

I came to in a room with cement block walls. The newly painted walls reflected the dull light shone through a single window. The lower bunk of the bed on which I was suspended was held together by a flimsy metal frame. Across from me and next to me were two wooden desks resting on a bare floor, each held up a bookcase and a tarnished brass lamp.

Aside from these things and the shared closet my new accommodations defined austerity.

Hoped I wouldn't have a roommate. I wanted the extra distance. Hoped administration ran out of bodies to assign. Sometimes people got cold feet, didn't show up or were admitted at the last minute to another school of more importance to them. I caught sight of the luggage on the top bunk and knew that was not going to be the case. I would have a roommate. He was coming with his candles. Candles lit in devotion under a decorated crucifix, bowing his head to pray. Justin and I had our misgivings. The Christian couldn't see much my way.

My music bothered him. Some days it would give him headaches and he'd have to wear the cross that hung around his neck on the outside of his shirt. He would stride in and out of the room rubbing the cross and muttering. After I went out he would light a row of candles to calm himself which only pushed me away more. I'd open the door and the miniature flames would beat nervously, shade across the void walls. It seemed like he was closer to the devil than I.

That was only a small part luckily. The days were new otherwise. Things were turning the way I hoped they would. It was the thick end of a hot and sunny summer with still great range. And the school was especially large, enough to get lost in. The way I liked. I didn't want to be at a place where I would stand out. I only wanted to blend in and the anonymity was comforting, like a stranger rubbing my shoulders. Class time was all that interrupted these perfect days. I craved still more freedom. I didn't want someone assigning me tasks and expecting results. I resented it and would do things that felt to me like I was hurting those who would dare toy with my time. I enlisted in some general education courses but couldn't get interested. Most of it was tired, things I'd learned earlier. I began to drink. Came to explore the local barrooms or usually just found a friend of similar mind. The alcohol filled in what was before hollow and temporarily halted an overactive subconscious. I once drank to take the edge off before an exam. I was mistaken and the booze did not clear the way for the right answers but only made me feel ridiculous until I thought of the act as a taunt.

Friday evening I was anxious, whole place felt so hot. The walls of my room were warm to touch and the air was even hotter. To move was to sweat because of the humidity; everything required more concentration to do. Guy I just met told me I could stop by his place; family owned a house not far away. It was in an area popular with the faculty. Imagined vine covered facades, turrets with their cones looking like unattainable rockets.

Put on different clothes, started over by myself. Walk was longer than I thought it would be down a lot of dark side streets and gravel alleys behind homes in the old section. Eventually, I would hear the din while its source was still hidden.

People everywhere. Scattered in gangs on the lawn or up on the porch and stairs. Someone was waving from the far end of the long wraparound. It was Jim. He'd seen me coming down the walk and as I drew closer he mouthed something, pointed to his drink, then in the direction I assumed was the bar. I traversed the broad steps that lead up to the stately structure, excusing myself when necessary, going around the islands of bodies. He was busy so I went indoors, among more guests, got a drink, returned outside. I looked for Jim where I had seen him at the far end but he was still talking intently. I put my back against one of the supports and took a long drink, grateful to have something cold.

He was in great demand so I went inside to have a better look. People enjoying themselves in his large house. I cast my eyes about admiring the woodwork and the open rooms and the carving on the deluxe staircase. The place effused warm light and kinship.

She said she knew me. I thought for a moment but couldn't remember. Tried to get me to go back to how the two of us did meet.

Before I could say much she had taken my hand.
"Are you coming?"
No goodbye for Jim.

Good to be out of the smoke and clamor but now the hot night dropped in. The air a tough draw and without current and what was normally in motion seemed to hold. But it was still better to be out in the dark. The fresh air acted to quiet me and I saw her for the first time, noticing her in what I can only say was closer to full potency.

She glided beside, her height crested just above my shoulder. She wore a serious yet contented expression. She maintained a serious pose but I saw the hope in her, and so she kept to herself when others were passing by.

"My name is Leigh."

Said she wanted to stay with me.

I told her it's alright.

Walked down a more and more sparsely populated path. I looked away, trying to avoid her eyes. How did she find me? It wasn't important but I thought hard to remember something that might tell me. Letting me in only because some door had opened in her life. Something recent. A decision she had made quickly, an idea whose time had arisen. Today she knew it and I was there. I went along with my surprise girl.

She was alluring with wavy black hair long and full to her shoulders surrounding delicate cheeks, soft eyes. She seemed clean. Lonely.

In my room I saw her clearly. Everything about her in front of me was shown to me. The glow from the small desk lamp was enough and I could see her very well. She was what I thought, body lean and compact and strong. Simple clothes. Faded white jeans and a powder blue tee. No need for anything shiny to make her seem like more.

Her shape was a smooth I had not seen. Like stone carved by water. She had muscles that were relaxed now but her skin was drawn tight all over. What's this? A girl with muscles? And her skin new and brown, so soft it was as if I couldn't touch it, my fingers would sink into it. She liked the feel of the sun on her, said so looking at me through her accomplice eyes, deeper than the skin I couldn't hook. And I realized her hair was also a shade of brown and not black. I could see it then in the light and the difference tickled me more.

Slowly reached for her wanting to try her on. Took my time so she would drive closer. She regulated my movement not being used to me.

She came toward me and I waited but she only wanted to help me with my shirt and her hair covered my face while she leaned in.

Door creaked behind and someone else was there. I looked as my roommate stood without speaking. His emaciated frame burned itself into my mind.

Our eyes met and he stepped out. I turned back to Leigh who only moved behind me out of view.

"No one's home where I live so we can go there."

Jerked our kicks on.

Trying to ignore the heat again, sound played in the soaked air going under the lights.

I remember how I felt in her room. A woman's room. She lit a candle and her colorful things illuminated in a fugue-like spectacle. Air tasted cinnamon on my tongue while cerise and shadow played inside my eyes.

I stood transfixed by the door then went across the tiny space to an area of floor beside the bed. When she saw I was set sat down beside.

We removed each other's clothes and fucked there on the carpet. My knees burned raw. Penis coated by a clear glaze. I didn't want to wash it away. A female did leave something behind.

Sun arose, wax all gone, burned away. Room and her hair again like cinnamon. We were tired, acting lazy like lions full in the shade. It was morning and I'd stood on top of it as long as I could.

Walked home in the white heat wearing the clothes from the night before. I had no energy and took a shower, tried getting dressed, went back to bed.

Saw Leigh two days later in her room.

Just showed up again for more water.

My hall was not really a hall at all, but many shoddy one story buildings end to end or three deep by more than a thousand feet. The hall's administration building and dining area were at the east head. And there was a simple music studio in its basement. Each separate space housed about twenty. All whose money was last in got the roughest quarters.

I befriended a wild one named Mitchell Cotto who lived down the row a few buildings. He had some energy around him that cracked always, like he knew something or had something everyone else didn't. Many who paid him just a glance couldn't see much. It required an active second sight to detect his air. I couldn't stay away because I enjoyed his distinct outlook and I watched to see what he would do next.

He was a gloomy girl special. Got the kind who were breaking up with daddy. Cotto's pretty musing face and twist of wolf hair made him a big prize.

Mitch was from a wealthy part of St. Louis. He really loved his mom and talked about her all the time. But he couldn't find his dad and this imbalance wore through him unevenly, making his fireworks. I overheard him speaking with his mother once and it was as if he were speaking with a sage. He was so concerned and selfless in the way he did it. He had a lot of reverence for her. I was curious about their relationship and it didn't bother me but I secretly envied their closeness.

We didn't have a great deal in common, but like I said, felt a strange pull toward him. Another reason I came around was because of the yellow racing bike he would let me ride sometimes. We went tearing around on that motorcycle of his at every opening. From the beginning he told me to hold onto his waist very tightly. I didn't listen because it seemed strange but I never knew anyone like him. I soon realized it was for my own safety that he wanted me to do it.

It took only one time for me to comprehend how serious he was, on a certain afternoon that Mitch was going incredibly fast, making the land a blur.

"Hold my waist tight!" he would yell over the wind rushing and the motor pounding. I just shifted in the seat and bent closer to him. We were leaning into a long curve and at the end of it he jolted the engine with enough gas to almost send me skipping across the pavement. My upper body heaved backward and my legs rose trying to go above me. It was horror as I was sure I was going to come away from the narrow seat and be tossed into the brush, at last hooked a thread of his jacket around the waist.

Mitch didn't turn around or slow down or acknowledge what happened in any way. His behavior told me I just needed to understand. If you want to ride with me, hold on, I'm not going to take it easy because you won't listen.

He showed me how not to be afraid and I learned to break through to the place where before I couldn't. Riding like that became a way to face what was chewing inside. To confront the part of me that till then had me stifled. I loved going fast, the act became a compulsion. Those empty roads were now to become solace.

Mitch and his women, twisted and too complicated. Never understood, slept alone but I knew peace. He did not get this about me and would on occasion exert a little pressure. He'd introduce me to someone and it would go on for a while but not long. I guess I just didn't share in his kind of refuge. Not at the time, saw what he offered were slippery glasses of water to drown the heat or sink me. So much happening anyway, nicer to only look on.

He was seeing a girl regularly named Andrea. She had long legs, short brown hair and the most delicious face a girl could have. Andrea was unmatched and I fell for her right away. Mitch treated her well and I knew there was not much of a chance but I also knew that he got bored easily. So I waited. Under the circumstances I didn't feel bad about wanting her. Mitch would soon move on. Besides, I heard adults say before affection at a young age was just imaginary.

I was sure I must possess a depraved spirit though. Mitch was a friend. Our tie was loose but there was no reason to undo even part of it, so I would wait until he had clearly lost interest to make it seem less diabolical. Somehow I knew he was looking for a particular kind of girl and that she was not it. Fine. Not much hurt for anyone.

♥

Andrea's lean form radiated beauty. She was an irreproachable little lamb. So wonderfully naïve. And who is naïve? I ignored the voice.

> I chose her,
> And she not me
> So it had to be
> Unlike the last,
> Don't you see?

A few days after I had rather obviously made my intentions toward her clear, I sneaked into her building. She lived in a high rise adjacent to my sweaty little ranch style abode. *How did people get in on this*? I clambered up the immense concrete steps to the entrance. When I was close, I could see a mature woman of about fifty waiting for me outside the door. It was late. She must get paid to watch the comings and goings after dark. She was much overweight seated on the metal chair. She saw me, shifted in the seat.

"Can't go in. No male visitors after ten."

I had never been referred to as simply a male before. I knew nothing was going to convince her to let me pass.

"I didn't know visiting hours had ended."

I apologized and walked back down the steps.

I went to the rear of the building and found one of the doors there to be off its latch. I knew the girls came and went through the back when it was convenient. I slid inside and made my way up the stairwell. The sound of my presence ran all through the chamber.

I was breathless after going up the six flights and tried to quietly open the heavy door and enter the corridor without being noticed. Orange safety lights illuminated the hallway at that hour and creeping around in the unnatural coloration got the impression of being somewhere off world. I continued until I stood outside Andrea's door then put my head in close and listened. It must have been near midnight. There was no sound coming from inside or anywhere on the floor really. If she was sleeping it would all be ruined, I'd feel foolish.

I was relieved to see a number of lights on behind her when she opened the door. She had been working on the floor in front of the bed. There were papers and books scattered everywhere. She was surprised but happy to see me. She asked how I had been able to enter the building. I didn't answer but instead walked past her and looked around. She had a quizzical expression then just started to enjoy me being there.

I brought a bottle of sparkling wine and thought I might take it out of the book bag. She liked the idea, plunked to her knees on the floor in front of me while I worked on untwisting the foil.

She was grinning, found new energy, said she would drink right from the bottle. I'd fish out two picnic cups anyway. The opaque plastic cork popped loudly into my hand, aimed away the neck to be sure before filling our glasses. I tapped hers with mine and took a sip. We talked and she got drunk from all the bubbles. The bottle ran dry and I'd enough to make me bold so we leaned toward each other during a silence.

It wasn't like I expected because I held her up too high and didn't really want her, just wanted to have her. Though it still felt nice, I was surprised at the revelation. Plain Andrea was who she was and just then did I realize. We talked a little more and sat on the floor facing each other with our legs crossed gazing at one another in the middle of the night.

The clock was showing half past five and I had to leave. She gave me a hug then put me in the hall but her eyes looked down before the door clicked shut. I went through the corridor soaked in orange light hearing all my sounds made big against the hard space. The whole world slept as I opened the fire door, went out where the sky bombed my eyes with iridescent blue in the day's beginning; saw no one else completing an epic calm.

Much of the week couldn't leave my room. Sick from a bug going around and it made me so weak and despondent I couldn't do anything but rest. Schilling from up the hall showed up now and then to see how I was doing. He brought food and different drinks that I was sure his mother had given him when he was ill. Thanked him for it but it really didn't matter because I couldn't swallow much of anything. He'd sit and I'd cut him short, asked him not to spend a lot of time breathing the same air.

Andrea came with me to a party at a mutual friend's house Friday. I picked her up in a borrowed hot rod and we went out of the way including a couple of stops at places she told me about as I drove. She was shy toward me but spoke to everyone else with enthusiasm.

Our friend was making some noise to celebrate his birthday. He had to do it himself he said. Eventually we parked in front of the house. I went around to Andrea's side, took my hand as she stepped over the curb. I knocked on the front door and could hear the activity but no one answered so we went in. It was a large white house with lots of room downstairs possibly from the lack of furniture. We called out, followed the music to the second floor.

Found Will. He welcomed us, painted smile; a drunk motherfucker. Shook my hand using both of his then hugged Andrea good and tight kissing her cheek. The two of them started talking but he did most of it then he realized I was still there and offered us a drink.

He set up three glasses, waved his free arm around while he poured. He splashed in some ice then capped the bottles, held out what he'd made. Andrea and I thanked him, each took a glass then he whapped his into each of ours without warning laughing outrageously.

Will wanted to toast our being there, raised our glasses officially. He was too happy to see Andrea, got excited about something, began to trance her, I made no effort to keep up. I visited with people nearby. But when I turned to look for Andrea and Will again they were not to be seen.

I ventured down the hall hoping to catch a glimpse.

He's with her somewhere I thought. A person like him almost had to force people to listen. And getting her drunk because she's so beautiful.

I couldn't concentrate; good deal of time had passed since the two of them disappeared. I began to look around the house. I searched all over the huge place but did it nonchalantly so no one might guess how I felt.

I opened the door and they were there amid the smoke and the debris of another messy room. She was sitting almost on top of him with one leg across his thigh and her eyes were closed and her head back while he kissed her neck and the side of her face. Andrea held a burning joint in the hand dangling over the sofa.

Didn't feel much of anything but sick. I think Will saw me but didn't recognize me in his condition or didn't care. Andrea appeared to regard him with indifference but she was relaxed, not thinking about me so I slipped back out.

I went for the car. Just wanted to forget all about the stupefying sight.

The motion sedated me, driving around in the dark. Finally let the car go, walked home.

I wanted my bed. Lights were off when the telephone rang.

"Come back."
"Why?"
"She's thinks you left her."
"Yeah."
"She wants you."

I couldn't sleep ignoring it. I didn't have the car and would have to walk.

Dressed in the same smoky clothes, began the nearly twenty minute gait during which time I had to remind myself not to act on any animal impulses.

Didn't knock when I arrived. Everyone upstairs anyway. Went quickly to the room where I had last seen her, right there being loud, behind coated eyes.

"What happened to you?"

I looked at her while she squirmed at me for some answer.

"Did you leave me, Joss?"

"No."

She jumped up.

"You shouldn've left."

She tried to look into my eyes.

I began to doubt whether anything she'd done warranted my leaving.

"Can we go?"

Saw the burn marks where she had been sitting.

I took her arm, hung it around my neck, she didn't have her legs and was almost falling. She mumbled something but I couldn't hear. I didn't want to agitate her or shock her system but judged I could leave her there or carry her. There were still a few people around, looking on as they will. I got her to the door of the room then placed her midsection across my shoulder, resting like a shot deer.

"Goodnight Andrea."

Will rubbing his face.

I braced her with one arm behind the knees and marched out without looking at any of them. Andrea laughed, made odd noises with every step I took. I was relieved she was not having a fit, arguing with me or kicking. Prayed she was not going to piss on me.

I guess in her bliss she was able to forgive her treatment. She might not have been that easy had she simply been crushed with booze and not smoked anything.

Once we were outside she pressed me to put her down. The evening air smelled sweeter and I was happy to have her walk on her own. Amazing what a different atmosphere can do. I set her up and she was steady then I made ready for what I might hear.

"What are you doing?"

I watched.

"Why are we outside?"

We made toward her building where she would go to sleep after so many flights, each bathed in orange light. The streets were bustling even at that hour but Andrea kept quiet and was almost beside me. I made sure to walk slowly and not to get too far ahead. Sometimes she caught up to me and tried to lean her head on my shoulder. But she couldn't match step for very long and would lose her brace.

We were about half way when she wanted to stop. We'd been following a path through a garden surrounded by some of the older lecture halls that was dotted with flourishing trees and shaped hedges. There was a round iron table with two chairs under one of the trees close by. She asked me to sit down and wait for her, would be right back and not to follow.

The night was old to me with its plain darkness and I longed for it to stop. How much more is there? I sat alone and leaned my head on my hand, waited bored beneath a far a-way moon. Andrea was gone and said she'd be back but I couldn't be sure.

Wasn't I foolish to have expected it to be different? But the disappointment still grew inside without regard for what I may have known. Vanity made me believe I should have what I wanted, tried to will it so while not appreciating that such a flimsy hut is the first to blow apart. The lesson was somber but the memory of her mouth with mine would al-ways stay.

She appeared out of the dark like a seam in it had been o-pened up for her to be presented.
"Ready?"
"What was that?"
"Nothing."
She acted as if she had no idea. I choked back my irrita-tion then I understood. I just never knew it could be done that way or that she'd want to like that.
The involuntary notion to hold the pretty ones up so high died that night. Keeping the belief was exhausting, didn't want to carry it anymore. Now I could see her, someone like me with sizable troubles of her own. I stood up to get going.

I left her at the entrance of her building where the woman was sitting alone waiting for overdues to roll in. I offered goodnight, going away for the second time.

Mitch and I took a ride along the river going toward Soldier's Town. It was an early fall afternoon and the sun shone brightly on the fiery yellow leaves shaking way up in the trees. There was an abundance of color in the midst of change accompanied by air that had some bite and its coolness made the landscape seem sharper and clearer. And despite its frosty harshness I liked the wind the most. With it rushing past I felt ahead of everything. I wiped away the tears from the corners of my eyes as they tried to keep themselves moist against the cut of the breeze.

We turned onto Soldier's Town Road after finding its almost invisible beginning and very quickly we were at the foot of the great incline that led to the overlook. I leaned into the slope as the bike humped in low gear.

I never knew of the road till Mitch showed me. Think he must have come upon it riding alone. As we approached a particular section I understood why it attracted him and hoped he knew how to handle it. We had gotten out of some nice jams riding together before. And we seemed protected like so many of those who wanted to risk but this was all different. There was just a single lane visible only in short lengths because it kept disappearing behind the tall corn stalks in the fields bordering each side. This, of course, made it impossible to see what was coming ahead. I didn't want to think about it. When the road bent it practically reversed so there would barely be time to react in case of a bad mistake.

Whoever built it must have imagined the horse and carriage were meant to stay and I wasn't sure even with Mitch's look.

Again that faith with no effort and I held on, never closing my eyes when it was too intense. We exploded through each turn and during those rough parts my being shrunk down. Just a little trick of the mind to keep me from thinking about what I'd miss. If I cared for my life I must be sane after all. That idea comforted me! I think I smiled! Apprehension disappeared because of any wish to die.

Mitch tore into the curves with everything he and the bike together were capable of. Sometimes one of the foot pegs scraped the asphalt below as we dipped and swayed up then down between the high stands of dry corn. The sound it made was a horrible screeching and if it were night I know I would have seen a pile of sparks. The turns were one after another and the road made no sense but I got used to the rhythm and the speed.

After the tireless pitching and leaning and sheer deliberateness all the road opened up into a straight and Mitch twisted the throttle to bounce up the front wheel. He was saying, 'I won!' He had. Lived to bargain again with the Soldier.

Stopped for something to eat, sat on the edge of the walk outside a filling station.

"Did you know Sandy died last week?"

"Sandy Donaldson?"

"I just saw him."

"What happened?"

"Not sure."

"What?"

"He was out on Soldier's Town, way behind. Modified an old café style into a nice racing bike, wasn't really used to it."

"Yeah?"

"They all met up somewhere but Sandy never came. They waited, thought maybe he'd taken a different way, trying his new bike."

"That's it?"

"Somebody called the police."

Mitch tilted back for a sip.

"Don't know if they found him that night or the next morning."

"Wow."

"Went off an embankment."

He looked at me.

"Lotta trees. Hit one way up, goin through the air."

We sat there, neither of us saying anything. I wasn't hungry anymore, just looked out at the road. A car almost sped past but braked strongly in.

Sandy was ready to graduate in the spring. Electrical Engineering.

Breathing in and out got a lot more valuable since one who held so much promise just disappeared.

Mitch and I jumped on again to ride down along the back ridge.

"Busy tomorrow night?"

"No."

"Like to go with me?"

"Where?"

"Dinner."

"Oh."

"Should be pretty good."

"What do I have to wear?"

"Suit?"

"Seriously?"

"Yeah."

"Okay."

"You're all set."

Waiting.

"What do you think?"

"Sure."

"Good."

She laughed.

"Anything else?"

"Gotta buncha work."

"I know."

"Hmm"

"Always."

"So what time?"

"Need to be there at seven."

"What about six-thirty then?"

"Yeah, about six-thirty."

"Six-thirty."

"Yes."

"Okay."

"What color is your suit?"

"Navy."

"I have something that'll go great."

Only wanted to have Leigh undressed again.

Justin and I were tired of living together.

He returned to our room after being away for days.

Housing told me changing was done under extreme circumstances.

"Could move you in with Vic."

Vic's original roommate left for home.

"I can get my stuff."

He seemed uncertain.

When I came to Vic's door with a load of clothes the man from the housing office was there.

"You're going fast."

"It doesn't feel that way."

"It usually happens differently."

"You talk with Vic?"

"Yes."

"What did he think?"

"Prefers living alone."

Vic's cheeks were fall apples, thick golden blonde hair.

He opened the door slowly. I dumped clothes in a chair.

"Here you are."

He didn't have much say.

The housing man stayed a minute.

Vic was leaning on his hands against his desk as I passed by him to get the rest of my belongings.

He showed me where I could stow everything. Had even cleared a space in the closet, gave me the lower bunk. It helped a lot him being easy. We wanted to get to know each other. The afternoon was sunny and the bright light shot through a window.

He loved music, showed me some examples then after so long in the room we wanted to leave. Brought a couple of chairs, placed them on the grass at the other end of the building where the sun was unblocked.

♣

Shilling had a chair; shadow gave my eyes relief while he set it up.

When I returned with some water Mitch was there, motorcycle was at the curb. Sat in the grass with his legs folded. Vic held a pack of cigarettes, shook one loose. He took the joint and lit it, breathed the smoke deeply, handed it over. I never tried, turned it in my hand. New smell and not my cellophane cigars.

"A little more, uh."

Held out the joint for Schilling. He took it, inhaling for seconds, reached toward Mitch who said no. Again to Vic and I. Schilling expelled a white cloud like a pipe when the engine's cold.

Drank some water, dripped down my face. Mitch wanted the water, offered some to Schilling who didn't care for it. Mitch began to tighten the cap; Vic took the container before it was all the way down. I leaned back to trees the size of oceans, autumn entered inside me as a golden pulse. Vic had a cigarette, traced his jaw.

People in a truck I'd never seen. Mitch went over. Leaves spiraling downward like odd shaped pinwheels. He stood with his friends at the truck. Schilling reached for the water.

"What's going on?"

Vic laughed.

I stood to go over.

♣

Mitch talked with the driver. The other two let me play with the dogs in back. One a yearling English Pointer, others were Redbones.

At my urging, dogs jumped out, lured them toward Vic.

Saw the dogs coming and sat up.

Sniffed, back toward the truck when the driver called.

I followed after, admiring them before they were loaded up, speeding circles, panting in back.

Andrea got a hand on one of the dogs before the truck pulled away. She and Mitch started speaking at the curb.

She leaned into him but he was back against the bike. Glanced over at me once, I waved but she did nothing back. Mitch listened thoughtfully seldom looking away but really didn't seem enticed. I knew she was happy to see him, touching him occasionally when she joked. He crossed his arms and just then she walked away. Now waved at me.

Mitch lay on his back, put his hands over his eyes.

Riders came, what he needed to coax him away.

"Friends?"

"I asked them. Be too cold soon to do anything."

"I'll go."

Vic too, Schilling remained.

Mitch fired the engine, other riders whose faces I couldn't see behind their visors lead the way. Recognized the bikes though, all metal and shine, like inside a jewelry case.

Trio pointed west, gobbling up country roads till we were farther out than I'd ever been. Warm air swept into us and blew past us deep into the valley.

"We'll just keep going!"

He didn't reply and I couldn't see his face. It was always ideal to dream in such a way. *What if we did?*

When I asked Mitch unreasonable questions he got quiet. His boundaries, still liked to try and push him out once in a while.

Rested in a clearing atop a long ridge, overlooked the entire valley, little figurine town in the distance as evening came.

Vic started over, lit a cigarette.

"What do you think they're doing?"

I recognized the pick up, dogs out and running. Each animal going from person to person, begging a throw. An unearthly noise as they quarreled with each other. Terrific growls deep in the throat, almost shoved Vic out of the way to see. Other mutts on the ridge didn't get along with those hounds. One of the mutts bigger than any of the others, mean from a crouched position with fangs out at one of the Redbones. Both owners knew what was coming, tried stopping it. Mongrel ready to attack as the weaker dog approached with his head lowered. Hound was too close, got nipped and thrown over for his good nature, went to the weeds crying.

More cars and a truck brought girls who began jumping from the back before they were at a stop. Once the girls were out of the way the driver spun the truck peppering everything with stone.

One girl found a saliva covered tennis ball, tried to hit her friend and missed, bounced into someone's drink. The girl covered her mouth but still laughing. She went after the ball, said something, walked away embarrassed.

The girl with her friends went over to a fire behind the truck that belonged to the locals. Big blaze from a pile of sticks, took Vic with me to introduce ourselves. Sat down next to the pointed flame, asked about the dogs, what did they use them for? The girls sat on the tailgate, giggling under a blanket, looking like nymphs in the jumping firelight.

After a few drinks I was on my way to the weeds, saw Mitch wrestling with someone in the dust over the bare ground. Both struggling to remain upright, had each other by the shoulders. They soon stopped with no apparent winner but I could tell each thought that they had won as they smacked away the grime, rejoined the milling spectators no longer cheering.

Among the foxtail, pissed in the direction of the lights, looked back to them by the fire.

Mitch and his friends seated with their backs against a car under the stars. I counted the orange dots drifting in front of them.

"What did you see out there?"

He was drunk, I pushed off him.

Took a seat by the fire, got the scent of what Vic brought. Dog resting, bothered him with a stick till he came over. He and I played tug for a minute but neither had the desire so instead I scratched his ears, he just lay down.

A girl in the truck poured some of her drink on the head of one of the locals. He stood to shake off, tackled her in the truck bed as she squealed. Somehow she managed to soak him again, sprinted away, had to use his own shirt to dry off. She slunk back toward the fire, celebrated in the bobbing glow. I petted the dog, gazed at the writhing girl and maybe her unpracticed moves. Completely embarrassed, ran to her friends.

Mitch and his on their bikes, one sprinted into the road, down it a ways. None to race so he came back.

Flames low, all the stars above, someone asked if the big bright one might be a planet. Most slept. Mitch next to an uneaten plate of food. Vic in the truck with the girls. Tucked a dirty towel under my head couple of hours before daylight.

Gave myself plenty of time. Picked up the suit from the cleaners, made arrangements for a car. In exchange for a few bucks someone always willing to loan.

Unwrapped it, put it on. Forgot how I looked as a mannequin.

Realized in the car I was going to be too early, drove across town, started back once the clock wore down.

Six-fifty. Left the car at the curb. Went inside to see what was keeping her. Couldn't stand it any longer.

Her voice carried, door was open.

Couldn't decide which dress.

"What are the choices?"

She held a black cocktail dress, swung slowly on her fingers.

"What else?"

A similar dress but dark blue.

"Wear the black. No one'll notice we're a shade apart."

"Black?"

"Yeah."

"Go outside," she said.

Little engages the mind while waiting.

She appeared.

"Okay?"

We got to the elevator, car at the curb.

"We're already late."

"So they'll miss me."

"Which way?"

"Stay on this."

We drove north until she told me where to turn. The place wasn't too far away but hidden from sight at the end of a long asphalt driveway which eventually circled in front of a squarish building clad in speckled blue granite. It stood by itself and was surrounded by a tremendous green, sprinklers still going. The finery out of place in the river valley.

"Builders and faculty will all be here."

Her event.

Doorman directed us.

She disappeared all the time, came around out of breath.

"I have to keep moving but come along."

Leigh stood next to who she was looking for till he noticed.

"Joss, Anson Kess."

"Joss? Nice to meet you."

"Anson is helping evaluate the bids."

"Are you in the business?"

"Many summers in my father's."

Looked at Leigh now that she'd fixed me and Anson up.

After eating people gradually excused themselves from the dining room and found their way outside or to the soft chairs in the lounge. A group of older men spat cigar fragments and drank iced brown booze. Once they all laughed in unison from the low part of their bellies and I almost began to laugh with them but wasn't affiliated.

The night passed quickly, a trick of time. When Leigh found me I was with the elder builders. Could see it was all over for her and that she might want to go. Had this way of pushing in to get attention. Didn't get to hear anymore of yesteryear from the men.

Away from home almost half a year. Fall session to come to a close within weeks. Time that had passed seemed like it belonged to a single unending day and night due to a sustained frenetic pitch that blurred all seams.

Pressing demon that had made a home inside finally rested. Nothing to call him forth. Traces resonate through me in the form of dour singing but a great deal of the fear and panic had subsided. Some kind of carcass though staying on. Remainder there in most everything. Stuck far away in my guts, certain to rise sometime.

Didn't forget Anson. Visited him. No intention of moving in, liked having another place to go.

Felt welcome, volunteered on occasion. Lots of activity, so lent a hand.

Borrowed equipment from the music studio at the hall. Took most of what I needed, let the custodian know, bring everything back in a few days. Didn't oppose me, thought it would be fine. There was a strange feeling I ignored. My deliberate manner always a mixed blessing.

Moved the equipment with an old pick up Anson provided. Unloaded, spent an afternoon connecting, disconnecting wires. Someone else was going to be handling the operation, showed him my changes, he understood. He said I should get paid. I just wished him luck.

Still plenty of time, went to a discount store, got a few items, coffin nails for the cook.

Took my time in the village, stopped for some food. No hurry to get back, when I did girls were there.

I didn't change because I wasn't done yet, I wanted to frame the day up over the night. Stay the same, soaking in the anesthetic of an afternoon. Tip top the way it treated me and dropped me where I was.

House filled up. Didn't get too involved with the central hum. Laughter of the women, responding well to our set up.

Music worked, only had to show him twice what I'd explained. Wasn't easy to get used to.

I talked with one of the girls, surprisingly open. Beautiful, hair thick curls, must have taken hours. Dress too, anyone would have thought we didn't belong together.

I stood out in my common clothes, everybody else had ironed, she didn't care or mention. Reason enough to stay with her.

Felt happy to be there but when it ended I was glad too. Wanted to go. Said I would pick up the equipment another time, thanked him or her, went outside.

Walked along the street with the mild wind in my face. One of the last mild winds of the season I feared. Heard loud noises, bangs, a voice suddenly elevate, watched them on their front porch.

Continued toward home. People darting out, excited on a busy night. Paths were full and the crowd was sponging up what they could before the cold came. Be like a warning, slow us down, bring on the bleak.

I sat across from Mitch who seemed to regard me with distaste. What's the matter with him? Refused to tire myself imagining. He kept his distance, talked to those around me, only looking at me when I spoke right to him and even then he didn't wish it. Someone made a joke about the missing equipment then I knew. Looked at Mitch staring at me accusingly. I didn't expect that kind of reaction from him.

"What's wrong?"

Mitch kept eating. There was another joke and everyone laughed except me. I didn't know what it was about and mostly ignored them but it also meant I had to get everything back to the studio right away. Saw he and the others thought I intended to keep what I'd taken. Explained why I took what I did, didn't believe me though, wasn't like him to care.

Unseasonably warm, elevated me as I walked. Paid those at breakfast small notice as they sought to discredit me, cast doubt. If they wished to make a game they would need to look elsewhere. Couldn't believe Mitch succumbed to popular opinion. It was due to his certain individualism that he and I spent time together at all, wasn't sure how to take him after what he'd shown me.

Made the effort to retrieve the equipment though didn't think it would do much good as talk goes, at least till time passed. They would think that since I had been found out I was anxious to right the situation and return what was missing. They thought they knew the truth...so I would have to give up a profit.

No one was around or they were eluding me. I walked for something to eat but didn't know what to have.

I started back at dusk, already a couple stars out big at the bottom of a glassy blue sky.

Vic wasn't there and I didn't see anyone else nearby. I pushed on the radio, lay in bed.

The alarm banged, jumped up, made ready like I enjoyed it. Washed and dressed, still a bit damp under my clothes, too early. Trying to be quiet, not wake Vic until there was a knock at the door.

"What?"

A boy stood in front of me, cowered and stuck out his hand. I took the paper from him. It was an appointment reminder with a day and time filled in. Same day and the time that morning.

"What's this?"

"Housing wants to see you."

"Why?"

"I don't know."

"Not much notice."

He shrugged.

"Go soon though."

On the top floor there was a directory and placards on the wood paneled walls with arrows pointing the way. Followed these around to the left until the right door.

The office smelled aged, too many spoiling decisions, approached a woman seated behind a writing desk in the reception area. She looked up at me when I was almost to her.

"May I help you?"

Offered the paper showing the appointment.

"You'll be seeing Mr. Ingram. Please have a seat."

She handed the note back. I acted like I understood what was happening. No sooner did I sit down than his door swung open, must have been aware of my arrival and was in the reception area now with his fingers on his hips.

"Mr. Carlsson?"

"Yes."

"Come in."

Went before him to the unlit office.

Sat down in a red leather chair, half a barrel.

"Things going well?"

"Think so."

His office was dim with only gray light coming in by a top window. My eyes had to adjust to see him in his darker clothes.

"There is sometimes a housing back up."

I was staring.

"Do you think you might be interested in living somewhere else?"

"I don't know."

"We're offering those who want a chance to leave. That is, a chance for some to live outside of university supplied housing within their first year. It's a chance to break your agreement with no penalty."

"No penalty?"

"No."

"Haven't thought about it."

"Your request for a new room assignment caught my attention."

"It did?"

"Are you happy where you are?"

"No, no."

"You've also had a few violations."

"Yep."

"What do you think?"

"What do I have to do?"

"You would have to use the break to make other arrangements."

"Okay."

"Just sign the forms I have here. You're paid through the end of the current session. The full year agreement will simply be wiped out and you can start again wherever you like."

"No more obligations, everything will be fine?"

"This has nothing to do with your status at the university. I only know you'll be happier elsewhere."

He waited.

"I would like you to sign."

"What is that?"

"It states that you agree to the terms of what is taking place."

I was looking.

"Only the things we've talked about, first page releases you from obligation."

"Alright."

"Just one more."

"What's this?"

"The second page states you agree not to seek housing with the university in the future."

"So I am being asked to leave?"

"Part of the agreement."

He pushed the letter over the desktop's inset leather terrain. I signed without reading. He gathered both papers together in a file.

"You'll have something soon showing the changes."

"That it?"

"Nothing else. Now remember, you will have only until the end of the session to remove yourself from the premises."

I nodded, having lost interest in what he was saying.

I was startled at the turn. Don't think I felt rebuked but been given a pass. I owed them nothing and could move ahead.

Went down the hallway past the other offices whose doors held in place frosted glass where none could see. I gripped the rail, descended trying to decide what it was I would do.

Ashen light wasn't hiding, realized the job of finding another home might not be difficult. Knew I wouldn't miss living in a row.

♠

The session's end conjoined with the season's. The week was solely for finals and no classes were going to be held. If your last exam fell on Wednesday evening you were free to go after and had the rest of the time for your own. As it went, I would be stuck till Thursday morning then go off for winter break until the start of spring session about four weeks away. I searched the ads during any free time but had found nothing yet that was going to work, lots of crazies hawking only filthy boxes.

It was a day without color or meaning whatsoever. Steely columns of expanding gray flew overhead and were set up in infinite rows attached to the heavy ceiling of an alloyed sky. The force of the wind pushed along the oblong shapes while its calamity cut their leading edges at sharp angles making them point in the direction of their path.

Little dry leaves clung to their bones by brittle glue, upset at every blow. From the pathway I could see the once luxurious lawn surrounding the psychological sciences building had turned from rich green to a deflating tan. The staid canopy shielded a smaller sun and a serrated wind moved among it all.

Have you found anyone?"
"No. Thought so, even put down a deposit but he never came back."
He stopped to laugh.
"Do you want to know where we are?"

I'd be sharing a bedroom with him and two more were in a second. Double sinks in the bath, kitchen and living room were one in an open space. Cost was two hundred a month plus one quarter of the utilities, about twenty five dollars. I knew the building, noticed it from the walk before. Modern stone structure better located on a wider street.

"Like to see it."

"2B on the second floor."

Receiver slid off my ear.

Again to the weather.

Aluminum mailboxes in the lower floor breezeway then up the stairs to the second or highest level. Each entry faced the open air. And on each level in a section there were only four units.

"Mentioned there's two other guys but they aren't around right now. Probably like to meet them before you made a decision."

Room enough for two personalities, my own bed and desk. Looked then at the bathroom, other bedroom, the living area.

Stopped in the kitchen.

"What do you think?"

"Good."

Door swung open, came an unusual looking dude, sinless girl behind, reserve which changed the room.

Him with dark thick hair, five foot seven maybe. In shoes she had him by a little, both watching with enormous grins.

Suddenly Brackman didn't exist. Focused my attention on these. Heard Bob's voice murmur the introductions. Strange one's name was Colin, by him his girlfriend Diana. My reason for being there was expressed.

"It's a great place."

Diana had gleaming pale eyes.

"Nice to meet you. Just had to pick up something."

He went hastily down the hall. The rest talked for a moment before Colin returned after getting what he came for.

I wished them a good holiday.

He opened the door.

"Hope you take the place."

Colin pulled her and they stepped out.

Brackman shut the door.

"Any questions?"

"How much again?"

"Two hundred."

"What else should I know?"

"Nothing right now."

Leasing office was in another block building to the left and opposite. On the way I searched for a reason my application should not be accepted. I crossed the street and pushed open the heavy glass door.

A lone woman behind a counter. She asked me to wait while she pulled the file.

She came over holding a copy of the lease in her rightful hand.

"You're going to be replacing Mr. Tiles."

I didn't know.

"Like to begin on the first."

"January first?"

"Yes."

"We can't remove him from the lease but we can add you on a sublease."

She mined a drawer.

"You may fill out the forms on that table."

Slid out my ID. Didn't know what she would do. Social Security was worn, never had looked genuine.

I completed the contract; she gave me back my license.

"You'll need to wait five minutes."

I sat in the sage loveseat.

"Here's an extra key."
I handed her a check.
"There's only a single copy of the one for the mailbox."
If there was anything else I needed call the number on the receipt.

Phoned Bob from the old room. I had a key so he didn't have to wait.

Passed Mitch on the sidewalk with a girl.

"Where are you going?"

"Leaving here."

The girl's presence made me feel in peril.

"I'm moving to an apartment."

Thought I saw pity in his face.

Still surprised Bob wasn't there. Felt like an intruder, arranged clothes in the closet, on the bed I knew was going to be mine. It was the middle of the day and no one was there. Colin on the road, other guy seldom about, stayed with his girlfriend I understood.

Belongings I possessed had been brought over. Left the key to my room on top of the desk. If there were more papers to read they could mail them.

I thought about Ingram, so many like him in the area for whom life is such a rigid thing growing out of an overdone practical side. Constructive order is necessary somewhat but they had let themselves be tricked.

In anger I would say they possessed inflexible minds that were limited by superiority and intolerance. Enjoyment found only in extolling the meager pleasantries of some old fashioned guilt ridden idea of virtue: self restraint, unhappy repetitious work to foster incurable resentment, and so on. I would continue to view them as narrow minded and empty, as my years allowed.

I set about to the discovery of life on a starved bent, this was virtuous as well. I needed to satisfy some longing. This was the best way to live.

We did not want to know each other, them and me. Couldn't do more than uneasily tolerate the other. I saw them as busily conjuring up ways to impede my fought for freedom and also remember wanting to turn the advantage, maybe by seeking out their drunken and attention starved daughters since it wasn't really in me to kill.

Their stern adherence to rule only pushed me harder. Isn't that how it goes? In my life I had only begun to lean against what might be considered the common view.

I was still troubled. How can a person be alive and yet seem not? Had they seen what I am seeing and found a better way?

In the faces of those I am referring to I would have seen compassion with empathy, some compassion, at least understanding. No, they were incapable of something as immature. To know the feeling of a racing heart and blood pumping through taut veins true as ever. Being so very alive that the air around is charged with rising electricity and blue wonder! And knowing beyond all reservation, what it is to truly live, to have a sense of it! After all, when the moment's passed, they could say that they had lived and would always be right.

Perhaps some of them had thought about this but were not able to hold on. Their early vitality was fleeting or uncomfortable so they chose to ignore their natural impulses, keeping most everything hidden.

♠

After exploring deeper my new surroundings, placed a call to Leigh. She said she had just arrived back and was exhausted.

I asked if she had plans to return home for the holidays and she said she did, going in the morning.

"Do you want to ride together?"

"I'd appreciate the company."

Felt the need to get away, allow the flurry of activity to steep in my subconscious. I agreed that I would meet her in the morning at her room.

Entered the hallway passing excited faces. Leigh's door was open and I found her crouched on top of a suitcase.

"Shit."

Noticed me in the threshold.

"You're just in time."

I placed my solitary duffel inside.

"Yeah. What do you got in there?"

"It's quite a load. Gifts for my parents, sisters, my niece, all my clothes."

"Okay, stand on top and I'll try to zip it shut. Are you sure you have everything?"

"I'm sure."

"We only wanna do this once."

She started pushing and jumping on the bloated luggage while I strained to get it done up without tearing apart the zipper.

She pounced above me like an angered troll while I puffed my cheeks and turned red attempting to coax the zipper around the fat bag. The image of how this must look made me laugh, stole my strength.

"Yeah!"

"Okay, now you can carry it down."

"What else have you got?"

"Still have to figure that out."

"So where is the car parked?"

She told me where her car was located, suggested I bring it around the drive in front of the main entrance. She explained that they were allowing people to park there temporarily for loading.

"Would you like money for fuel?"

The check from the sale of my car arrived sent by my stepmother, still hadn't spent any. She got my asking price.

"Joss, help me carry this, the ride is free."

Hide something in her purse later.

"I'm going down."

She was in thought as she sorted the items.

"Where're your keys?"

"Top of the refrigerator."

Picked them up with a jangle, went amid frantic girls and traps of orphaned baggage.

While riding in the elevator it occurred to me how much trust I had placed in my stepmother. Upon the sale she could have kept all the money.

I left the luggage at the curb while I brought the car around. Looked at the gigantic suitcase when I wheeled up, got it in the trunk. The weighty new burden rocked the suspension. A man shook his head sympathetically. Stepping back it looked as if the car was on one knee. The attendant appeared, explained to her we were loading, up and down a few more times. I had to leave the keys.

Leigh made progress, stack arranged by the door.

"Take any of that you can."

Seemed good performing regular tasks for her benefit.

Leigh came out of the elevator as I was returning from stuffing more into the car.

Don't know why she couldn't go light, now she inspected my packing, everything she wanted was on board, she still had to go back up.

I stayed with the car, got a cigarette, lit the sweet tobacco and took a heavy drag. Going home. First time since summer.

I blew out.

Nervousness formed a knot.

I hoped things could be better this short time.

Leigh and I veered into the gravel drive, got out to the misting rain. She watched me with her arms folded because I told her I could unload my own luggage.

Sour day, stinging air going to make snow. I yanked my bag from the filled trunk trying to ignore the high nervousness.

"Everything alright?"

"Thank you for the ride, have a merry Christmas."

"You too, merry Christmas."

She hugged me.

We waved as she backed out, I didn't sprint for the porch, looked at the door in disbelief.

The days tripping along, stale. Nothing had changed; the usual holiday time unease. I watched television in the basement and smoked cigarettes in the nasty cold. My favorite spot was under a couple evergreen trees next to an unused woodpile against the southern wall of the garage. The lower limbs provided a natural shelter above the soft floor of needles.

Out there I usually observed the atmosphere from a squat, liked to think of my new life somewhere else, reminded me it was all right to leave.

Noticed most of the logs in the pile nearby had turned rotten but not the curved remains of an oak barrel stacked on top. And the now useless steel hoops were leaning against each other sloppily at the other end.

Why couldn't the people inside know me? Just a poor blend which couldn't go up for sale. And as strangers we seldom spoke and we did not inquire.

During meals speech wasn't more than ordinary responses, keeping inoffensive. No one wished to spark an increased trial. The combined family naturally sought calm after years of none. We tiptoed all around the brink, nobody wanted to fall. It had taken months to stand up and so the fear of relapse brought such distress.

Suffering, everyone knew if we could get through the time together easiness would be restored. I saw they wanted to resume in the security of their routine. The family holiday of feigned closeness that is now a cliché. Nothing wrong with wanting to go back to certainty.

I made friends in high school but had lost touch. Little parts of the past which were never revisited. So time outside the house was spent going to movies with my older stepbrother or drinking in one of the many area bars. I began to understand I wasn't part of them anymore but stranded in hope or courtesy or necessity. Haunting a place pretty lonesome, resentful. Time at the house like waiting for a train to pass when you're running late.

My stepbrother gave me a ride up. Using hard drugs had rearranged him emotionally so conversation in the car wasn't comprehensive. He communicated in his own new speech. To see him you'd have thought him an example of well being, the mostly inapplicable grin. Mixed up galoot was a hairbreadth from his own devastation. I didn't worry for him, reminded me I should be away.

It was the first holiday without someone walking out. No late night calls to a trusted savior. No sleeping in the car or at a friend's house. No belongings strewn over the lawn. We made it.

I hauled my stuff upstairs and set it down in front of the door of my new apartment.

Colin heard me enter, came out to help drag the stuff in.

"You're here early."

"Yeah, came back, wanted to see Diana too."

I continued down the hall.

I flung the load into my room thinking I would put everything away later, returned to the living room where Colin was now on the sofa smoking a cigarette, watching football highlights with the volume up too high. He seemed like he was comfortable with his legs crossed and the arm-rest supporting his bent elbow.

I sat at the opposite end, sighed. He looked. Smoke caught by light sneaking in had him wrapped up.

"Good," he said.

"I couldn't wait to get out of there."

He watched the changing picture ten feet in front.

Mentioned how it had gone the last couple months, how I got out of supplied housing. I was beyond their view.

He told me about growing up on Lake Michigan, how much he enjoyed sailing. He came to school because of expectation and had no idea what he wanted. I had a feeling he was not going to class. Diana was everything, said he'd figure out more as it came.

It was a new outlook for me. Impressed me. I liked his sureness. His peaceful air was so unknown, faith it was going to be all right. I found this troubling. I would not let my lack of understanding get in the way of our becoming friends. We enjoyed an instant familiarity, prompted us to share a lot of what we'd seen.

I saw much of his fulfillment came out of an ideal boyhood and days at the shore.

There were fires on the beach next to great water in the company of beautiful, natural girls with welcoming candy faces.

He boasted of his prowess sailing the small lightweight catamaran boats that he and his friends all had and I believed every word, fairly obliged as he told me. I took from his expression that his skill at manning these craft must be awesome.

He described riding the waves of a blue lake with a southerly burst in his sail. Sometimes the wind was so strong the boat would stand on its hull's edge almost vertical and he would lean strong against the rigging of the harness trying to make her steady but the force was so much he'd be thrown into the exploding cold.

The rigging of his suit once became tangled around the mast holding him underwater. He worked to free himself but the thin cable was tight and holding him down.

"A friend came to check. Saved with a second to go."

"Wild story."

"Unbelievable!"

"Were you thinking about dying?"

"Of course."

"I don't wanna go!"

"Sailed back."

Shook my head.

Both laughed.

The day went on like that.

Hadn't had anything like a best friend in a long time and many of the people I'd met now seemed estranged.

Outside, darkness came, still only the two of us in the apartment. I must have been dozing because I felt the sofa move inside of a dream. I blinked and saw Colin was gone so I stretched out full length. I awoke with him standing over me, asking if I wanted food.

"Sure, do you want to go out? Nothing in the fridge is mine."

"Bobby and Mark are buying tonight."

"I'll buy food tomorrow and pay them back."

We had a meal on the table in the dining room, the space between the back of the sofa and the refrigerator.

I thanked him for cooking, offered to do the dishes. He left the room.

He sat down again at the table, poured out what looked like dry lawn from a container.

He then removed two cigarette papers from a pack he had with him, seamed them together. He reached into the blue-grass with his thumb and forefinger, sprinkled what he took away in the crease of the tissue, going wordless as I watched.

He reached into the pile once or twice more till the a-mount in the crease was enough. He picked up the stuffed paper holding both ends using his thumbs, middle and index fingers, began to roll and twist the whole construction, licked the outer edge.

"You like to smoke?"

"Only did it once."

"Well, you'll like this. Good for these kinda nights."

He finished the shaping.

"Go ahead."

He took a lighter and flicked it at the end of the joint. The fire engulfed the twist of delicate paper. He briefly inhaled then hurriedly blew out the flame.

"Goin good now."

I felt at ease. His habits didn't alarm me. I more or less trusted him from the beginning.

So I smoked too, inhaling weakly. Didn't want to end up making that sound like a choking donkey. Colin watched me get high with an amused look on his face. I took what I could then gave up the white stick to his reach.

He took several more long draws then doused it. After a short time, I began to feel very relaxed, not mindless, but utterly calm, able to think and speak with different clarity.

♣

It wasn't that he was odd looking just unique looking and I guess good looking in that way. He was athletic and quick and alert. I didn't realize until years later that he was not right where he was. He fit someplace else. I couldn't think of where. It's hard to belong to something. When you're changing, you don't know where to go.

Sat with him at the table, spent the rest of the night telling each other stories from our lives.

We looked forward to each other's company. Neither was much involved with school and succumbed to such a complete diversion. I was doubtful of Colin's registration with the university while I was enrolled but usually not seen in the classroom.

Excursions into the bar scene. Colin introduced me to people he knew, collected. Colorful mix of waifs, musicians and bullies, most pretty humble, searching, never was I uneasy. Kids paying their own way for the first time.

Only one concerned me. William. Don't ever call him Will or Bill or Billy. I was told before the meeting.
    "Okay. William. I'll remember."
    "I don't want to make him upset."
    "Understood, fucking William."

Long after dark we made our way across school property, through the slum until we came upon a handsome building hidden in the gloom by sky scraping trees at the end of a silent street at the slum's edge. The lights on the structure's exterior cast their faint glimmer my way in a lonely stare through barren stirring branches prompting some stroking whisper that accompanied me as I drew nearer.

I followed Colin up one of the open air stairwells to the highest floor. We stopped in front of a door where my eyes fixed on the shiny gold numbers 410.

Huge man in the door, tilted my head to see all of him; expressionless face that saw with eyes that had no end. He and Colin only met each other's gaze and we were going inside. The two of them exchanged some words across the room while I just stood looking around. I had to ask myself why I was worried about being welcome.

The room behind me was filled with all gym equipment. Weights and dumbbells collected around a bench press.

I could hear Colin and William speaking quietly. William must have been seven feet tall. He wore a red tank and blue jeans. His height, bones wrapped with sheets of muscle, made it hard to glimpse him long. The tan face drawn tight over a jaw forced to grow to the size it was. His hair thick brown reaching his shoulders. He did not appear to be a stupid man. He was thoughtful of every word and though we did not speak knew he was most aware of me.

Sometimes they would laugh together. I could hear in Colin that it was strained and artificial, obviously was trying to get something.

I watched from a recliner close to the door. When Colin finally walked toward me he had something in his hand.

He motioned for me to follow into the room with the bench press and the dumbbells. Colin repositioned a couple folding chairs from along a wall to the sides of the bench which was supporting a loaded straight bar.

"Sit down."

I asked what was going on.

He formed a depraved grin holding up a gadget that looked like an acrylic pepper mill.

"What is that?"

He cackled as he studied the object.

"What's the matter with you?"

"It's William."

He gave me their conversation, how he couldn't get what he really came for but instead was welcome to any coke stuck in the little machine.

"What is so funny?"

"I can't buy anything, you know?"

Colin turned the gizmo in his hands. His face brightened when he realized exactly how much was still in there. He shook the cylinder and carefully scraped its walls until he was satisfied that it contained nothing more.

He collected the powder on a small mirror he had on the bench. William came in to see how we were doing and asked if we cared for anything to drink. He disappeared and I heard the noises he made off in the kitchen. He returned after only a moment with three brown bottles, offered off two of them, caps removed. Thoughtful, surprising behavior for someone who didn't appear that he would be.

William saw the amount on the mirror, quickly smiled.

"Always more than you think."

He went out.

Colin leaned over the bench, went to work making the powder smoother with a razor performing now with lucidity and seriousness and if anything more were humorous I saw this to be it. The direct light and white walls worked together to create a sort of a raw atmosphere and my eyes may have been playing tricks but in the brightness of the woebegone space the flakes seemed to sparkle mineral pink.

Colin made it smooth, separated it into long rows, thick and wide, filling the area of the smudged glass.

Using a short tube he made the first row vanish and after sat back in the chair with his eyes on the ceiling pinching his nose offering me the little pipe with his free hand.

I hunched over the bench to do the same then arced back reaching for the drink on the floor beside me at the same time giving the tube over to Colin who took a second turn right away.

When it was all gone and there was no more we sat on the metal chairs unearthly content, happy times for the brain. So we waited for the grip, smiling grotesquely at one another, drinking our drinks in the room filled with round weight.

Euphoria like my soul taking flight reached me and I coughed as it did and took another drink. But despite all of that or maybe because of that, I couldn't remain in the apartment much longer. I didn't know what I might be capable of anymore. And I didn't want to see how William would react to what he thought was intolerable.

"Let's go, don't you think?"

Colin was suspended.

"We don't want to wear out our welcome."

He uncrossed his legs.

"William is not what you think."

"That may be but I don't know him and I'd feel better someplace else."

Colin relented, my concern was sincere, he left the room. Alone I became aware how far off I'd gone. I felt ready to undress from my skin and escape to the outside. The great excitement in my head wouldn't last so I wanted to get going and enjoy it somewhere other than there.

Swallowed the end of my drink, moved out to the living room. Colin and William were talking. I picked up my coat and put it on by the lounger. Colin saw me, held up a finger then was coming over.

"Ready Freddy."

I smiled inside.

Colin found his coat and we made for the door. He yelled goodnight to William, I waved, we made for the door. How deeply human I seemed in this new landscape that had un-zipped and was pushing and pushing. Perfectly imagined and dropped onto a silly waiting world. We bound down the flights of stairs in the chilly air like fast cats just loose after too long confined. Snow began to fall while we were inside and melted ice cold on my skin and I could see my breath puffing playfully in front of me and I was sure it was some-thing I needed running out of me. And an all new exhil-aration arose in the sharp calm with snow drifting down. Through the dark and white we slunk around old trees and between parked cars on the black surface until we found Rock's.

♣

In from the cold, atmosphere staying me. There was an open area at the bar and we made ourselves at rest on the worn stools. Not too busy so we didn't have to shout to make ourselves heard. We ordered drinks smiling to some overdue knowledge.

The bartender delivered, slipped off our coats.

"Good idea coming."

The music was playing at the right volume, enough noise to be in tune with our nerve.

"What's his story?"

Colin laughed calmly.

"What did you think about that?"

"Strange."

He sensed I liked it.

I didn't ask how he knew William. There was much more to him which I didn't want to become familiar with, a giant who sustains desperation.

"I called Diana. Supposed to meet in thirty minutes."

"Great to see those eyes."

He was proud I thought she was darling.

When Diana arrived we got a booth. She had heavy winter gear wrapping her snugly. Her cheeks were red and her eyes glinted in the warm light like silver charms. Colin helped her with her coat then she slid in beside him.

"How have you been, Joss?"

She moved in her seat trying to get situated, became self conscious and that fantastic heeding girl reappeared.

"I'm alright."

"I hardly see you and Colin."

"You can have him back."
Her brow rose.
"Are you done with him?"
"Yep."
We laughed.
"I don't mind, the store's been busy."
"You were mad."
"Just jealous."
"I'm sorry."

Any sensation I had earlier was gone from the Kentucky punch. We spoke almost nose to nose till the place got a lot quieter.

Diana suggested we get going, take us in her car.

I said goodnight to my friends, the sound of Bobby breathing somewhere in the dark, quietly got undressed, pawed for bed.

I wadded my napkin.
    "I'm running out of money."
    There was a nice silence.
    "What would you do?"
    "Find some work."
    He held his arms up.
    "Don't worry."
    "I'm not."
    He was fatigued.
    We finished our food.

"Do you think you'll graduate from here?"

"Yeah."

"Me too."

Colin's mind was boiling. The relationship with his parents was good but he said he wouldn't ask for any money. He'd witnessed his sibling's appeals for handouts and refused to become like that.

Diana was around more as we slowed. A local, sweet tempered and accommodating, overly devoted to him. She worked in a gift shop across the river and wanted to be manager. They met as he was buying for another girl. Diana liked him right away. She fit with his homey side he said, although little about her wasn't fine. During her frequent visits to the apartment her soft beauty had not gone unnoticed by me. She came over one afternoon after returning from a trip to the Gulf of Mexico but when I opened the door it was to someone new, much more drawing. Brown skin, hair stained gold, contrasted her aqua eyes in a leveling way.

Embarrassed by my look.

She leaned against the counter with her hands behind her while she waited for Colin.

"Are you seeing anyone?"

"You mean do I have a girlfriend?"

She nodded.

"Not now."

"I have someone you might like."

"Really?"

"I'm serious. She's very nice. I'm sure you would have fun together."

I didn't care.

She spoke of her friend the way girls do about each other, nothing wrong.

"Bring her, I guess."

Colin came.

"Sorry."

He kissed her cheek.

"Colin, Joss and Amy might like each other."

He shook his head.

"I don't think its going to work."

Diana glared.

"Why don't you bring her over, Di?"

He turned to me.

"You'll know when you see her."

"Amy, like the plow horse."

"It could be great."

Diana already dreaming plans.

Evening brought a light snow. Diana had already gone and we sat in the living room talking to some music.

"He should be here soon."

Colin looked at his watch.

My stomach reflexively fell.

"Who should be here?"

Colin said nothing. I looked at Bob.

"I don't know what he's talking about."

"William."

Colin's voice was low.

"William is coming over?"

"Why?"

Bobby turned toward the window.

"You think we should have him here?"

Colin was annoyed.

"It's nothing."

"Why is he coming?"

"To bring me something."

"What?"

I received more silence. I let the subject drop. Maybe nothing was the matter. Everyone talked and drank and smoked cigarettes until I decided to go to bed, said goodnight as I stood up from the sofa.

"Good night," they parroted, their eyes followed me sadly as if I was abandoning them.

I sat on the edge of the bed to take off my shoes, Colin was against the door.

"You don't like it?"

"This is the best way?"

"I think."

"Don't wake me."

He laughed and went away.

I woke to the sound of excited voices. There was laughter and the anxious talk of those who do not know each other. I lay wide eyed on my back and knew William was inside the apartment. I waited until he had gone before I bothered with my curiosity at all.

When the pitch of the conversation dulled and I heard the door I heaved aside the covers and got to the window. I lifted a slat in the blinds slowly with only a finger then peered between to try and catch a glimpse of the figure who rattled me so much. And in a second a tall man with long hair broke into view who then straddled a motorcycle and began trying to kick start it just below. His coat was shining black and a knapsack was slung over his back.

♦

I watched the stranger ride from our lot before coming away from the glass. He rode away in the light falling snow. I hurried into my pants and went down the hall. Bobby and Colin were at the table laughing, pushing their hands in the big pile, feeling it between their fingers. They had drunk a lot, now eyed me haughtily. I watched as they continued to play in the sticky leaf the way many talk about running their hands through lots of cash.

Fell into a chair and handled some myself and when I looked up their eyes were stuck to me. Their anticipation turning to crazed laughter.

"Has to be funny?"
"Its okay."
Colin's light heartedness made no difference.
"Just one time."
"Does Diana know?"
"No."

I rose from the table because I couldn't be that close. They began to act soberly and worked putting it all away. Sorted quietly sitting next to each other and only kind of whispered when they spoke at all. I watched across the room with a-mazement then went to bed.

I was concerned at the attention it would bring. New faces coming to the door. So I began to distance myself. I saw Colin as too temperate and lacking the obstinate will re-quired by the risk, only hoped it didn't come to overwhelm him, wondered if I should have just given him the money myself.

I spent the weeks attending class, helped make a lot of the bleakness disappear. Saw friends I'd been neglecting, went to places I hadn't been in a while. Did what kept me busy and away, telling myself it must almost be at an end, Colin would have what he set out for, the apartment a welcome place again without the column of half hollow boys.

I visited Leigh but she wasn't alone, had Anson.
"Nice to see ya."
"You too, Joss."
Gone too long, hadn't paid any attention.
"I'm here if you ever need me."
"Thank you."
"Come over sometime."
"I will."
Anson smiled at this.

"Good morning."
I was still unfit for words.
"Everything's going well."
"Good, good."
"I have an idea."
"Another."
"You haven't really been behind this."
"I don't know."
"So I wanna finish up."
He shook his head.
"The only reason I did this..."
"Yep."
 His face still bright.
"That's what I'm leading to."
"Have a friend about three hours south, grew up togeth-er."

He expected an interruption.

"He'll take what I have left."

I stared.

"Would you like to go with me to see him?"

"I don't think so."

"We'll do that then have the whole night."

"I..."

He groaned.

"How do you wanna get there?"

"Rent a car."

"I'll see."

"Like to leave Saturday, wanted to reserve something."

He ate his cold breakfast, went to rinse the plate. I watched him finger scrub the residue wondering if I should go along, feeling some obligation. Usually I'd have helped with most anything he wanted but I had a chance to ensure it finished quickly, making the difference.

I didn't let him know till evening.

Even liked the idea of having the night he spoke of.

Colin held a car for nine. We stayed up drinking in anticipation of our early morning.

Sun was shining making it easy to get going. I went over to the window. There was a little snow on the ground. Gathered mostly in crevices, on the edges.

Put an extra shirt, pants into my duffel. I didn't shower or shave, just rinsed my face and hair. Colin might have done the same because I never heard the pipes but his head was combed wet.

He got on the phone for a taxi. In twenty minutes it announced itself.

"You ready?"

I looked around.
"Run!"

Swung into the beige sedan with our bags on our laps, yanked the doors shut.

"You guys're goin downtown, right?"

I handed over the address. Writing it so I didn't have to repeat myself. He looked at the scrap, subtly nodded.

Stopped in front of the agency, he gave the driver twenty who wanted to show his gratitude by carrying something. He just opened Colin's door. I went around and joined him on the sidewalk, followed him inside the office where I sat in the waiting area while he made whatever arrangements for the car.

"Bumped us to a bigger one, nothing smaller like I held."

We had been a little late.

"Nothing extra either."

He was proud.

He opened the driver side, popped the lock to my side.

We had our seats.

"Mmm."

I couldn't help smiling back.

"Let's go."

I pulled off my scarf and put it in the back seat with the rest of the stuff.

He let it warm up, slipped the large car into gear. The air out of the vents was still freezing.

The travelling made a life seem better.

The flattish land was uneventful, stopped for fuel, carbonated drinks. It was cold out, closed my eyes. As we got near he needed to study the directions written down with black marker on part of the newspaper. He turned the *State & Local* pages different ways.

"I'm gonna give him a call."

"Be right here."

As he jogged back I could see he thought he knew where to go. With the engine still running he planted himself hard in the seat and he abruptly shifted. We circled and turned left down a street I was sure we passed earlier.

Stood on the slippery pavement making jokes, breath clouds.

Colin put on his coat, slung the backpack. I followed. He had his sunglasses on, walked leaning forward as he was eager. A lot more snow there and the sky had changed.

We crunched through a layer of ice on top of the ankle deep snow as we sought the right building. The snow was grainy and had probably begun to melt then refroze. He saw the number on the door; we cracked and crunched that direction. He took off one glove, rapped his bare knuckles against the freezing metal. Whoever answered was no William, taller than me but a lesser frame, neat black hair, face of a blue jay. He put his arm over Colin's shoulder as they turned inside. I tried to relax.

After their reunion, Jeff faced me.

"Nice to meet you," he said.

He looked at Colin.

"You'll like him."

Back to me.

"Easy coming down?"

"Just the drive."

He was by the refrigerator.

"Good to see you."

He felt comfortable near Colin.

"Sit down if you want."

I sat on a sofa while they occupied the dining table.

Colin reached for his pack, produced a stuffed pouch.

He pulled the bag; put his face to the opening. Stood up, taking the pouch with him went to the kitchen. He opened a cabinet and removed a scale. He placed the package on the tray, watched the red number lock in.

"Still the same?"

"Yeah."

I rubbed my sharp beard.

We smoked then, shared a couple drinks. Colin, Jeff did the talking. I listened while they recalled adventures from childhood. Jeff's father ran a company importing some kind of building products and owned the apartments where his son lived.

"I have to work, though."

"You sure?"

"You can come back."

"When?"

"Hmm, eleven."

"See if we can get together."

We wandered into a cold land. Jeff skipped in the door, shut it fast after us. Snow was falling and noontime was gray as we set out over the frozen lawn to the auto. My spirit still high as we crunched and cracked through the hardened melt.

He unlocked the doors and we were in, winded at the close.

"What do you wanna do?"

"Find a room and wait till tonight. Watch TV, I can take a shower, get food."

He waved his hands in front of the vent.

"I'm buying," I said.

He was having little luck warming up.

The rear tires spun, I looked over at the building.

Threw my bag into a chair and fell on the first bed. He came in after parking, said he was going for ice. My eyes were closed, sleep an inch or two away. He took the wrapper from the ice bucket.

I was startled awake by ice landing in an empty glass, running water. He lay on the other bed to watch television.

"When you wanna eat?"

"No schedule"

"I'm not hungry."

"Wake me in an hour."

He leaned back.

He was quiet except for the television.

The nap was enough but made me listless.
Sat up to stretch.
  "How do you feel?"
  He was leaning back on his elbows.
  "Shower time."

I slid from bed and grabbed my bag with the clothes, shaving shit. Colin didn't move or look at me as I went past. Engrossed in a movie, smoking a cigarette. Big motel ashtray next to him. I heard him admiring the 1940's actors. Been a while since I'd seen him that way.

I would lean almost unaware against the tiling to let the water wash over me. The rest of the room behind all the steam. I stretched for the towel on the counter. Still didn't shave.

  "In there a long time."
  "You leave any hot water?"
  "Yeah, how's the movie?"
  "Fell asleep."
  "I'm ready to eat so whenever you're ready."
  He looked at the TV.
He moved around trying to locate his pack, unzipped the main compartment, wandered unhurried for a scrub.
  "Sorry about the cold water."

Sat on his bed in front of the television. It was difficult to resist the urge to lie down again. I unfolded some jeans and put em on.

♦

Moved to the round table in the corner of the room and pulled a cigarette from his open pack, with my legs stretched out made smoke animals and waited for dinner.

He emerged from the bathroom wearing one of the towels left by the motel. He walked over to where I was and picked up his pack of cigarettes on the table. After lighting he began to talk about how well he thought things went earlier. Relieved it went as he hoped.

"What did you think?"

"Jeff could have gone back on what he said."

"He came through."

"That's right."

He finished his cigarette and wished he was an actor on television while he got dressed. It was a different movie now. He slicked back his thick hair in front of the mirror then came up to me.

"Where're we going?"

"I've never been here."

"We passed the town on the way, has to be something by there."

We put on our scarves and wool coats and stepped into the blue, wintry night. The cast of pink from the streetlamps in the parking area highlighted the snow as it fell. The sharp air was reviving, vaporous crystal holding still.

Drove the direction believed would lead us to the small town we had seen. After criss crossing found something we agreed on.

"Smoking or non smoking?"

He held up his cigarette.

She came to a stop in front of a booth.

We hung the coats on post hooks, slid onto the spongy seats as the waitress approached.

"What can I get you two to drink tonight?"

"What do you have?"

"Do you want beer?"

"Yes."

She recited the list, he picked the last one.

"Two."

She nodded.

He felt he had to defend himself. He then looked away acting like he was miffed.

"Is that yours, is that you in the picture?"

"Of course."

He grinned.

"Can I see that?"

I held out my hand.

"You're an old man."

The place was dark, quiet with hardwood touches. Customers altogether were just above a murmur. The waitress returned with the drinks and told us she would come back in a few minutes to take our food order.

"Would you like her to light our candle?"

He twisted his lips.

I laughed.

Fresh cigarette in his mouth.

"What do you feel like?"

"Nice steak, maybe."

She came.

"Are you ready?"

"I'll have the filet sandwich, medium rare, with fries."

"Okay."

She took my menu and looked at Colin.

"Let me have the pork chop plate."

Had her go over the sides, selected two.

She went toward the kitchen. We smoked cigarettes, rubbed our chins a moment in quiet.

"Why are you smiling?"

"Oh, Joss, come on, you know why."

The waitress put the plates down, picked up empty glasses, marched away. Rest of the night still lay ahead. When the food was gone we leaned back for a smoke.

"I know a couple places."

I looked at him.

He smeared out the short butt.

I finished my cigarette too before we paid. Then we unhooked our coats saying goodnight to the waitress on the way out.

Night brought some cold air. We wrapped our coats around tightly, drew up our collars, hands deep in pockets. Our warm breath came to life before us as rolling clouds while we plodded the streets in the moist cold, in the floating down snow.

Colin knew somewhere only ten minutes on foot and with the temperature we were thankful it was no farther. I usually loved to walk and could tolerate about any distance but when the bitterness outside began to chew on my ears I thought about little except the relief that came with being somewhere warm.

A bar with a fireplace in the center of the room. Good place to sit between the bar and game tables. I ordered two drinks while Colin patted himself down searching for a pack of matches.

We drank slowly into the enclosed fire. Within an hour the room was almost completely full with the adventuresome. It was Saturday night. We played pool as a team against other pairs and mingled through the native gauntlet.

After such a crowded place we wanted to hear music. Left the warmth and certain atmosphere for a loud club. After just a while on the street we found a beehive spilling over with girls dancing with each other. The volume nicked my skull. He went closer to the floor. I stayed by the bar. Sexy girls just out for their own.

They circled the bar during less popular songs, something to look at since we couldn't hear.

Colin was drunk and dancing with an unattractive older girl in front of me who was also gone. Her hair drooping with moisture, sick eyes. He held his glass up and took a huge sip while she rubbed herself against his thigh.

We were stumbling ornery along the leaning sidewalk while others passed by exhaling their own breath clouds at us. Fate somehow guided us to the car because to me it was lost. He pinch flipped his cigarette at the curb making a tiny burst of sparks, groped around his coat for the keys. He found them but had trouble inserting it. Said his fingers were numb. I hugged myself waiting for the door. He got in quickly, turned the engine over, lit another cigarette and blasted the heater. Vents shot icy wind as he drove the vacant street.

I was hunched over to massage my head. I looked at him in the other bed. I was afraid taking a shower would induce me to crawl right back to sleep.

I was dressed and sat at the table. Pulled a cigarette from the pack I found in my jacket that I guessed got there sometime during the night. I leaned in, struck a redheaded match and touched the fire to the end of the injured cigarette. I held it loosely in my fingers and looked up only to notice the terrible light fixture hanging by a chain of gold links.

Sat under the builder special lighting and looked over the room. Slid the drapes partially and daylight cut through.

"Good morning."

He tossed the covers and leapt out of bed in one action.

He went to the bath and I stood up to open the front door for some outside air. It was another day of the same dark and gray, not much different from the last. I welcomed the nights for the reason they shrouded the seemingly unending overcast sky.

I put on my coat, walked into the dark light of late morning, quickly snapped my fingers and then spun around; forgot the keys.

Car was across the lot at a brave angle. I brushed away some snow to unlock it. Rigid leather gave me a shooting chill. Started the motor, shoved the heat to maximum. Got out to clear the windows.

♦

I smelled the late coffee. A woman watered plants around a window. Their television was fastened in a nook above the counter.

"Ready to go."

I nodded.

"Be twenty nine."

His wife moved around spryly in the window tending her indoor garden with a feminine watering can.

Colin was shaving.

"You pay the guy?"

"Yeah."

With his face hidden behind a mask of shaving cream and wrapped at the waist in a white towel he walked to the center of the room and picked up his pants that still held a belt. He plunged a hand into the pockets then asked where the hell his cigarettes were.

"I think I have them."

I flung the pack from across the room. He frowned as they went high and had to make a catch. The remainder were bent or torn. He glared at me as he carefully removed one and placed it up in his mouth. It wouldn't get smooth anyway he tried.

"Better?"

"Yeah."

"Please hurry so we can eat."

He nodded but would have ignored me.

"The car's warming up."

He looked at me like he may have enjoyed appearing such a spectacle and was going to begin a conversation where he stood.

I sat impatiently wishing that we had some more time away. School and I weren't in uniformity. Being alive was so much better than it had been. I felt pacified even without a goal. Behaving another way seemed like it could only take away.

We left the door ajar, key on the table.
Colin opened the running car, hot air rammed into him.
    "We're gonna burn up."
    "Forgot to turn the down the heat."

We drove through town until we found somewhere serving breakfast. It was Sunday so it was crowded. We gave our name to the girl and waited about five before we were seated. The table had a chipped and white surface in an otherwise completely white and black trimmed restaurant. The colors of our hunger it seemed.

We ordered pancakes, potatoes, coffee, eating our breakfast among loud talking locals then smoked cigarettes to finish. We refilled our cups from the black and gold dispenser our waitress left at the table with a dish of artificial creamer.
    "Sugar, please."
    I handed him the cylinder.
During the meal large snowflakes began to drift down. I watched them while I smoked with wonder. Sometimes the wind would become fierce shutting the door hard behind a person or rattling the large windows. The tempo was frenzied, making it seem as if it were coming from every direction.
    I paid at the register while he stood facing the glass door.
    "Still wanna go?"
    The cashier looked at me.

"It'll be okay."
"You can drive."
"I hate driving in this."

I came over to look out with him as I put away my wallet. He shoved on the door straining to keep hold from the force as it hit. He had to muscle it closed leaning into it with both hands and I had to squint my eyes because the wind made them water with its freezing edge. He caught up to me to pass me the keys while gusts bossed us around, spread our coats.

"Go to sleep or listen to music if you need to."

He didn't want to hear me.

It was snowing hard.

We strained through the slushy streets of the besieged town following signs that promised to lead us to the highway. Visibility on the main road was much worse. He said it was because there was nothing to block the wind, only open and flat. Many were pulled over. He acted nervously, shifting his legs and arms. I stayed in the far lane at maybe forty-five, fifty. After a few dozen miles he relaxed.

The wall of white was still fighting. I looked across the bleached real estate to see something solid but it was all lost in the great brightness. Our car lurched from the force of a strong blow. We continued to see groups of stopped vehicles. I drove on unwavering. Colin smoked and stared out the window with nothing to say.

The rental agency was going to shut down. An anxious clerk offered to let us use her telephone to call a taxi for a ride back to the apartment. The company though said there would be at least a two hour wait. We had to keep the car another day. The woman applied a new rate because of the situation.

He slept away the day into the night.
I just looked often to the storm.

Book II

"You want one?"
"Long day."
"I got this."
He waved the bottle by its neck.
"Somethin goin on?"
"Nope, on sale."
I watched him.
"What have you been doing?" he asked.
"Library."
"Go good?"
"I don't know."
"Not really bad, though?"
"Not really."
We sat at the table.
He'd received a serious looking letter.
"I'm thinking of quitting."
I wanted to take the letter.
"You don't need to quit."
"I'm not sure this is where I should be."
"Why don't you just wait? I thought you decided you were gonna graduate?"
"I can't decide if this is something I want to do."
"A lot of people aren't sure."
"There has to be a way you can put it on hold."
"I've been doing that."
"You need more time."
He smiled uncomfortably.
"It's not the money?"

"That's some of the problem."

"Are you planning on marrying her right now?"

"That's not it!"

He couldn't' believe I asked.

"What then?"

"Don't feel like I want it."

"Here or any school?"

"Any school."

"I'm afraid I'll sound like your parents."

"I don't think so."

"So what do you think then?"

"I'll stay till May and might move in with Diana."

"I knew it!"

"That's not it."

"C'mon, Joss, you know me."

He stared at me painfully.

"But that's not it."

"Because that just seems crazy."

"We don't know."

"You know its harder if you don't finish."

"I've thought of that."

"Maybe twice the work."

"I'll find something."

"Things will always be fine. I have a great family. My dad, my brother's doing great. It's not something I even need to think about. You'll see."

"You seem like you know."

"I do."

"All right."

"So let's forget about that, okay, just relax and have good time, let's enjoy."

"That's all I wanted to do."

He took a big drink then walked over near the music.

"Let's just keep things moving. You and I are always going to have a good time, you know. We can't worry about any of that, we just have to keep moving. That's what you and I have to do all the time because there's too much of all that other out there."

He nodded and got a breath.

"Too much, all those people wasting whatever gift they had. There's too much of that, Joss. All the other people want to be like you and me, so don't listen to that crap. Feel how you're supposed to feel. C'mon, Joss, let's not even bring that up. You know I'm doing the best I can. I'm never going to let myself down. I'm never going to let my family down. You know that. They're always going to help me do the best I can. I don't have to worry. And Diana, she doesn't have to worry. Everyone's okay. I can't even believe there's something to worry about! I've come a long way. I can't stop now. What about you, you'll never stop, I know you, Joss? C'mon, you know you'll never stop. I know, I'm sure. What are we even talking about here!"

He shrugged, drained the bottle of beer, went to the refrigerator for another.

"One for me."

"Where's the opener?"

He went clanging impatiently through the drawers.

"Gone for a while now."

He opened both bottles on the edge of the counter banging on them with his palm.

"Well, I just wanted to see if you knew what you were doing."

"I know, I appreciate it, Joss, I do."

"It's still some time away."

"Hmm."

"Where do you think you'll…?"

A knock came.

"Come in!"

He yelled shutting my mind.

The three girls who lived across the hall came over to begin the weekend. Colin and Bobby knew them. I didn't know them but had seen them before. They brought a bottle of wine and a carton of beer.

"You can put that in there."

He pointed to the fridge.

We exchanged greetings then they went into the living room to drink their wine.

Before we could restart our conversation there was another knock on the door.

"Come in!"

Diana peered around the edge with a big smile.

"Come in, come in."

"What's happening?"

She didn't reply, instead looked at me.

"I brought someone."

Oh, no. I stopped breathing, envisioning her misshapen face.

"Well hurry up, come in."

His mood was still fallen.

Diana entered, behind her this very attractive girl.

"Joss, this is Amy."

She and I exchanged timid hellos.

"So what are you both up to tonight?" Diana asked.

"You're lookin at it."

He took a drink, frowning.

I could see Diana was annoyed.

"Colin, Amy would like something to drink."

Her eyes opened to help with the point.

He sighed but faked a better tone.

"Absolutely. Amy, would you like something to drink?"

She was smiling.

Thank God she had a sense of humor.

"Anything'll be fine."

"We don't have much to choose from."

I became amused.

Colin felt Diana's eyes so he didn't look at her.

He handed each girl a bottle and I noticed the beer was from our neighbor's lot.

The day he was having.

He relaxed a little, got the girls laughing.

I put two of our fresh bottles in the neighbor's carton.

Amy stood up from the table and put an empty into waste.

"Get me the rum from the cabinet behind Diana."

She was in an unfamiliar place and self conscious and so did as he requested. She flipped open several cabinet doors before finding the right one while Colin continued talking about something else with us.

Amy came over to me with the rum sitting down playfully in my lap. Colin put down a cigarette then reached across the table and took the bottle from her. He put the cigarette back in his mouth, smiled crazily, unwrapped the rum's neck.

"Reach behind you for that glass."

Diana didn't stop talking while she turned away then to him with the glass.

He poured about an inch of rum.

"Anybody?"

Amy leaned her head against mine.

"You first."

Diana watched.

He lifted the glass to his mouth, drained it. Poured another, handed it to Diana. She took it but made a wrinkled face as she drank. Her expression made me laugh and told me what to expect. I didn't care for straight liquor. I wouldn't have chosen rum. When she was done he took the glass then poured another.

"For you."

I curled my tongue at the chemical taste hurting its way down. Slid the glass over the table. He again filled it, shoved it Amy's direction. She took her head from my shoulder and drank without making a face but finished at a leisurely pace that annoyed him.

The bottle ran empty. We were extremely drunk, oblivious to our surroundings until I realized the living room was full of people.

I saw Bobby, Mark, a few neighbors, and some of their friends.

Amy kissed my neck softly. Only Colin noticed as she and I left the room, started down the hall.

We could hear chatter and loud music into the early morning as we lay talking. With the crowd gone I made my way out of the bedroom. The bathroom light was too bright and there was nothing to drink out of by the sink. I went down the hall and located a clean glass for some water.

The stars stopped bursting allowing my eyes to readjust to the dark and I went to have a look out the glass door while I finished the water. And there on the floor were two naked forms close together, no covers, just carpet under them.

I went to my closet.

"Everything all right?"

"Yeah, be right back."

By the time I returned the two were gone.

I stood in the living room turning the blanket when there was sound outside. I opened the door a slit, peered through. There were the naked squatters looking back. They were hugging themselves, shivering, jumping in place.

"Could we please come in?"

I couldn't get past my bewilderment so he eased open the door and brushed by.

"What are you doing?"

I tossed him the blanket.

He covered himself and the girl on the sofa.

"I'm Craig and this is CJ."

"She's here from California."

I still didn't understand.

"I'm a friend of Bobby's."

"Why were you outside?"

"When we heard you we thought we would drive home but we couldn't find the keys or any of our clothes."

"I don't see them either."

"No."

I started toward the back when Colin appeared followed by Amy who had wrapped herself in the covers from bed. He got a beer.

"Who are they?"

I just wanted to go in back without having to explain.

"This is Bobby's friend Craig and his girlfriend."

CJ looked toward Colin, nodded cutely when the blanket slipped.

"CJ, that's right," Craig said.

Colin looked at me.

"It was late and we were tired and…"

"No, no, it's no problem," Colin said.

"No problem."

I looked at Amy.

"What's everyone doing?"

She looked at each of us. First at Colin, then at me, and finally at the naked couple in the living room. Diana was completely clothed.

"What's going on?"

I didn't know if she was on the verge of tears.

"I came out to get something to drink and all these people were in the living room," said Colin.

"Why are you drinking, where are Joss' clothes?"

"I couldn't sleep."

"Night, Craig," I said. I pulled Amy's arm.

She curled up next to me. I could hear Diana in the hall.

"That was the strangest thing. Those two were already here?"

"Sleeping in the open with nothing on."

Soft laughing.

"We need to go to sleep."

"Are you tired?" she asked.

"Yeah. I need sleep."

"I guess I could."

"You know, your friends seemed comfortable, like they get caught at that sometimes."

"They're Bobby's."

"But you know."

"Sorta seemed like it, didn't it?"

"It's still funny to me."

"Yeah."

"Are you tired?"

"Pretty tired."

"Okay."

When I closed my eyes I pictured Diana's laughter.

The apartment began to stir by ten. I picked up a slumbering Amy, blankets and all, carried her into Colin's room. She squirmed but didn't start to squeal. Before anyone could stop me I tossed her onto the bed with Diana and Colin whereupon he slid out from under to the edge smiling. He lowered his feet to the floor, sat up, groggy.

"Good morning," I said.

He grunted and reached for the pack of cigarettes by the alarm clock.

Diana and Amy snuggled each other under the blankets both staring up at us. Colin lit a cigarette then sat with me on the empty bed opposite the girls. He reached over to the bed stand for the ashtray, placed it down between us.

"Had the strangest dream last night."

"Me too." His face was lowered, he rubbed his head.

"I don't know what that was," said Diana.

"Have you checked on them?" Amy asked.

"Not yet."

I decided to go see.

"Nobody. They're gone."

I took a seat on the bed again.

"I'm sure they left early," Colin said, holding his smoke an inch from his mouth.

"Weird."

"You say they were outside in the middle of the night? With no clothes?" he asked.

"Nope, not wearing anything."

He snorted.

"They were trying to drive home but couldn't find their clothes."

"Yeah, driving clothes?"

Nobody knew.

I found out later they wanted to make love outdoors but it was too cold.

"The kitchen is a big mess," I said.

"More than that," said Diana.

"Who were all those people last night?" Colin asked.

"Neighbors, friends of friends, their friends."

"We'll clean if you run for something delicious to eat," Diana said.

"But we have food here."

"No you don't, Colin."

He sat up straight.

"Joss, when you get dressed maybe you and Colin could go for something to eat."

"What sounds good?"

"Colin knows what I like."

Colin was moaning around the room in his maroon boxer shorts putting out the cigarette, pulling on a shirt.

"Oh, come on. I am trying to relax."

"You can relax when you get back."

I reached over Diana for Amy and helped her to her feet.

She and I returned to my room and met under the covers. I wanted to be with her one more time. I think she wanted to be with me too. But she was tired. I kissed her head to feet in the knotted blankets. She was mine, given to me, so I didn't have to leave a morsel.

We dozed then; eventually I slipped out of bed, put on some clothes. When I was ready I looked through the crack Colin's door made and saw that he too was fully dressed.

"Let's go," I whispered.

He motioned for me to come in and wait. He was talking with his dear Diana still in bed. She gave the guy fits sometimes but because he was blind.

Diana smiled at me over Colin's shoulder.

"I think Amy had a nice time," I said.

It sounded bizarre after I said it.

"I think so too," she replied.

We continued smiling at each other.

"Come on, Col, I'm hungry," I said.

"So am I."

"Where are your car keys, Diana?"

"Somewhere."

"Look over there."

Colin found the keys spilling out of her purse on his desk then leaned over and kissed her on the cheek.

"See ya, you two."

She tugged the covers and rolled toward the wall.

He and I walked to the kitchen.

"You weren't kidding. Look at this," he said.

"Going for food is a small price, don't you think?"

"What a smart guy."

"Well, don't you think?"

"Let's go."

We loaded ourselves into Diana's car. He drove.

"Everything all right with Diana?"

"Damn. Forgot my cigarettes." He searched every pocket to be sure. "Yes."

"You think?"

He made a grumble.

"What's open now?"

"Well, it's after two, so probly everything."

"What about Chinese?"

"Sounds good."

We parked the car in the lot of The Smiling Dragon on Traverse. Colin panicked as he searched for his wallet. He soon found it; we were able to get out then. After the cigarettes he wasn't certain what he'd brought.

"That girl last night, CJ, pretty good looking wasn't she?"

He was facing away.

"You saw that too?"

"What do you think has Diana acting that way?"

I nodded.

"Just seeing that girl was worth it."

"Oh, shit."

He stuffed his hands in his pockets, head lowered, still smiling as we entered. He was used to a cigarette so he just put his hands in his pockets.

"What do you want, Joss?"

"You been here before?"

"Diana loves this place."

"Whatever's good."

Colin ordered the food from a woman trying her best English. She smiled, nodded rapidly. It was a mystery how we got everything we wanted. Colin turned and walked over to where I was standing.

"Be about ten minutes."

"She tell you that?"

"Always takes about ten minutes."

We had a seat on the bench between the door and the bubblegum machine.

"Thanks."

He nodded.

"The food's good, you'll like it."

We sat there not feeling well.

"I don't have much energy."

He took a deep breath.

"Well, what a night."

"Woo."

"Are you hung over?"

"I'm not doin good."

I shook my head.

"Wanna feel better."

"The food will help."

"And the day."

"Maybe the day."

An old woman no more than five feet tall carried our food. Colin took the stapled sacks. She smiled and bowed and smiled and bowed. We smiled and nodded back then turned and I pushed open the door. The woman behind the counter was still waving.

"Must have been her mother."

"Yeah, I don't know."

"Is the food hot?"

"Feels hot."

"What about sauce?"

"They always put it inside."

"Soy sauce?"

"Inside."

"Couple packets or a lot?"
"Yeah."
"I like fortune cookies."
"Me too."
"Good taste after."
"Yeah, inside."

We stopped for cigarettes. And bought sodas too. God it tasted good. We started drinking it right in the aisle.
"Anything else?" the female clerk asked.
"Nah, this is it," Colin replied.
"Get a ticket for the lottery," I said.
"And a ticket."
"Five forty nine."
He threw a ten on the counter.
"Hand me that would you, Joss?"
He was trying to do too many things while he was driving. I handed him his drink when was ready. He was drinking, smoking, trying to hold the wheel. When I took the can back he looked relieved.

Diana and Amy were busy scrubbing the kitchen.
"We appreciate this," I told them.
Colin was unpacking the food on the table.
"We don't mind," Diana said.
Amy smiled but didn't look up, continuing to wipe the counter.
Colin searched the cabinets for clean plates.
"Where, Diana?"
"In the dishwasher."
"Oh."
"Bobby was here asking about his friends," Diana remembered.

"What did you say?" he asked.

"They left I told him."

"Does he know?"

"I think so because he laughed."

"Take a break and let's eat," I said.

The girls both dried their hands.

"What's for who?"

"Whatever you like," he said.

Diana looked at me, I smiled.

"Looks delicious," she said.

"Amy?"

She pointed to the barbecue pork.

I went ahead till she stopped me.

"Rice?"

"Some."

She nodded when it was enough.

We served each other, ourselves. Amy was quiet as she ate.

Most days I had only lunch specials so the meal was high living.

Diana and Amy cleared the table, resumed cleaning, Colin took the cigarettes from his shirt pocket. He pulled one from the box, tossed the pack to me.

He looked as if he were going to pop with satisfaction. I removed a smoke, set down the box. He held out his lighter and rolled the barrel so I leaned forward for the light.

He stood up, walked over to the sliding glass door and gazed across the parking lot to the street as he stretched his arms behind him.

Amy and Diana soon finished in the kitchen, went in back for a while. When they appeared they said thanks and good-bye.

♣

Mark rarely came around. He lived with his girlfriend for the most part and running into him was only a matter of course. He kept a little food on hand and technically shared a room with Colin. Some mornings Colin would wake to find him there in the other bed. Usually sleeping it off from a long night close by. He paid his rent on time and checked for mail sporadically. That's when I saw him most.

Mark angered quickly and wasn't that bright and it was easy to tell and he was ashamed of it. But that didn't detract from his meanness which he wielded from a rather bulky frame. His friends were just as rambunctious and dimwitted making all of them hard to like.

I was seated at my desk late at night when Colin came into my room clearly upset. He glared at me for some time.

"I had a lot of money in my room and now it's gone. Have you seen it? Do you know where it is? Jesus!"

Shook my head slowly.

"I'm sure you'll find it."

"I don't think so."

He was perspiring.

"Why?"

"I don't think so."

"What happened?"

"My money is gone!"

I wanted to comfort him like a son when he was broken up.

"Where do you keep it?"

"I have a small ceramic chest in my closet. Diana gave it to me. But it's still there. And the money that was inside is gone!"

"All of it?"

"Yeah, all of it."

"It can't be far."

He just grumbled lost in his agitation.

"Try to relax."

"I mean, it's just, man…"

"You sure it was in there?"

"Absolutely."

"Did you search all the other places you may have left it?"

"I already did that."

"You're sure you didn't leave it someplace else? Diana's car?"

"I tore everything apart."

He sat down.

"Anyone know about your hiding place?"

"I thought only me."

He was sitting on the bed with his hands in his lap despondent.

"This isn't a joke is it, Joss? You really haven't seen the money?"

"It would need to be funny for me too."

"I believe you."

"Then I just don't know. I don't know what could have happened."

"Do you think Mark, maybe?"

Colin's face grew sullen while he thought.

"You've never really gotten along. He's not really one of us here and sort of drifts in and out. I don't wish he'd come around more but he'd lose nothing much personally. Maybe it was the perfect opportunity."

"I don't know."

He crossed his arms.

"You might be right."

"Just be careful. And just watch out. The guys he hangs around with…"

"I'm not worried. I know one of them. He knows me."

Another spring. The still, constant cold of winter gave way to milder days. The nights remained cooler, sometimes the days too, and the wind began to blow, bringing the change. Heavy coats and jackets could be confidently discarded. Skirts, dresses and stuffed tees appeared on sidewalks as a good sign of the thaw.

The lawn in the square was trying to turn from sickly beige. So far it was only doing so in patches. A sweet aroma wafted in currents near the blossoming magnolia and pear trees whose flowers seemed to magically open at once each year to show off their thick red and rich white at the first sign of warmer weather.

My thoughts turned to what lay out from the city, the hot pitch top I loved to sail down. I rode a bus to town, over the bridge and river. Inside the dealership motorcycles were lined up in rows. I examined many, felt fluttering in my stomach. I spoke at length with the shop owner about different aspects of my favorites. He was like I would have thought, big beach ball belly, thick but tousled gray hair, impatient superior voice. Had some small town understanding of the world. Wore a powder blue golf shirt tucked into his jeans, opened the door to hack up something in his throat. He listened to me ramble, laughed sometimes at the way I asked questions but still followed me around the showroom making me feel as if I was his prey.

I told him thanks; he said if he could be of more help let him know. I didn't let on I had picked one out because I wasn't sure how I was going pay for it. I didn't want to buy something if I had to make installments. As I waited for the bus decided I'd call my mother. I was sure she'd help. She understood practical things, money, transportation, though bad with people, carefully knew practical issues. The sky turned overcast. I watched citizens on the bus, the swelled brown river as we went over.

No one was at home. I sat on the bed, sunless afternoon, remembered a time when I used to see my mother often, seemed long ago. I thought about when she used to send me letters on proper stationary asking how I was, to say hello. Sometimes she enclosed photos of just herself in front of the house, holding a dog or a getaway with some ocean in the background. Ridiculous. I still had a hard time disliking the photos. Kept some but got rid of more. She sent the letters for a couple years. It was as if she wanted to try for closeness. She, with her husband and my younger brother lived in another state. She had her own life to puzzle about. But I still wondered why she seldom came. With parents you would always wonder *why this* or *why that* to no good end.

"Hello?"
"Hello, mom, its Joss."
"Oh, Joss, how are you? Everything okay?
"Yeah, mom. Everything's fine."
"Oh, good."
"Well, how are you, Joss? What in the world are you up to down there?"
"I'm fine, mom, just called to say hello and to wish you a happy birthday."
"Oh, thank you."
"Sure."

"How are classes going?"

"Fine. Everything is fine."

"Do you have a girlfriend?"

"Nope."

"Well, there's plenty of time for that."

"How is Keith, mom?"

"Oh, he's good. He doesn't think you like him though, because he's only your stepfather.

"Well, you can tell him that's not true. Tell him we'll go walleye fishing this summer, that should make him happy."

"All right, I'll tell him."

"Is Aaron there?"

"No, he's with his friend."

"Tell him I called, would you?"

"I will."

"Is he doing alright?"

"Yeah, he's doing fine. He gives me a headache sometimes."

"Oh."

"He's young."

"Yep."

"But he has friends so I get a break."

"That's good."

"He and Keith eat a lot, and I'm always cleaning up or cooking."

"Uh huh."

"When Aaron's gone I'm not going to cook so much anymore."

"You won't have to."

"I don't think I'm going to."

"Mom, I wanna buy a car, maybe a car."

"Really."

"Yeah, I'm going to have a job soon and I'll need something to get me there and back."

"How much are you thinking of spending?"

"A couple thousand. Or three thousand, I think. I found something for about three thousand."

"Do you have some of your own to contribute?"

"Some, yes."

"I'll need to speak with Keith about it before I can promise you anything. He's the one with the money."

"I know. It would be a great favor, mom. He doesn't have to worry. I could pay him back."

"Okay, we can talk about that next time."

"Thank you."

"You're welcome. So, how are your grades?"

"Oh, fine. They're fine. I'm thinking about changing degrees, though."

"I thought you did."

"I was only thinking about it before."

"Oh, well, keep us informed."

"I will."

"Stay on track, Joss."

"Yes."

"You don't want to get off track."

"No."

"Okay."

"I won't."

"I love you."

"I love you, too, Mom."

"I'll call you in a few days."

"Okay. Bye, mom."

"Bye, Joss."

Colin came home, was eating a sandwich.

"Did you find your money?"

"No, but I have a good idea where it went."

"You do?"

"I can't tell you now."

"Well, I hope you find it."

"Will you be around tonight?"

"I should be."

I walked toward the door. His eyes never looking my way, staring through the paint and drywall into the studs over the sink.

I spent the best part of the day sitting outside the place that stocked all my favorite sugar. The sky still splotchy, warm enough but with heavier winds. I was in a chocolate cheese-cake dream as I watched my people go. Only one or two others ever hard enough to have a slice out there with me behind the knee wall.

Mark was in front talking on the phone, drunk, too loud with whomever he was speaking. He saw me, hung up with a bang.

"Why the hell are you telling Colin I stole his money!"

"I don't know."

"He said you told him that I was the one who took his money."

"Maybe later."

"Fuck you!"

"Come on, Joss! Come on, Perfect Man! What did you tell him that would make him think that?"

He was drunk absolutely.

"Did he actually tell you that I said you stole the money?"

"He said you told him we didn't get along."

He woozed up from the sofa.

"I did say that."

Mark was silent as he searched his limited resources.

"Did you take it?"

"Hell no, I didn't!"

He was pitiful; don't think he ever repulsed me more.

"All right, nothin to worry about."

Even he knew when he was being patronized.

"I've been busy all day so…"

I heard a muffled *fuck you* as I went down the hall.

Bobby was sitting at his desk reading.

"What's the matter with that guy?"

"He's pretty nervous."

I stretched out on the bed and closed my eyes.

When I awoke Bobby was still seated behind me.

I went into the bathroom and leaned one arm on the sink. I turned on the cold water, rubbed my brow bone with my thumbs. I could hear Mark bickering on the phone in front. Still seemed conflicted about whether he had taken the money.

He caught sight of me. He staggered a little, face covered in severe sweat.

"Sonofabitch!"

"Shut up, Mark."

He was standing there seething.

"You know you're too wasted, so take a break!"

I walked down the hall. My deliberate manner mounted its horse. I noticed the empty bottle on the counter.

"Why don't you relax?"

He staggered up close enough for his shoes to be touching mine.

"I won't, because U-R-A sonofabitch!"

I reached back, drove a heavy fist into his middle. The blow sent him back; he was down holding his guts.

"I'm tired of listening to you! You're makin a lotta noise, hardly even live here!"

His eyes reddened. I waited for him. He stayed down on that knee. The shot finishing its way through his system. I couldn't tell what he was thinking. I like to believe he knew he didn't have a chance. He put his hand out as a peace gesture, started to stand up.

I waited, he kept a hand up.

I turned, saw Bobby with his back against the counter, arms folded.

"You'll just have to pay it back," I said.

He was doing better, holding his stomach, leaning against the table.

I walked past him toward the hall when I heard the commotion behind me. Mark and Bobby were grappling on the vinyl floor. Mark was holding an empty bottle in one hand. I quickly pried it from his filthy fingers. I worked on separating the two still struggling. Helped up one.

"He tried to bust you in the head with that bottle when you turned."

I looked down to Mark.

"He couldn't get past me."

Bobby was out of breath.

Mark looked no worse, just sat on the floor against the wall breathing hard.

Bobby wore a scolding expression. He'd had enough.

"Thanks."

"You shouldn't have turned your back on him."

"Thought we were done."

"He had that bottle all the way back and was gonna to bust you in the head with it. I caught his arm and threw him down. Then he tried to hit me!"

He laughed a little.

"Thanks, yeah."

"Lucky I was there."

He was still breathing heavy as he remembered every-thing. Mark sat in silence, bottle alone on the floor. It wasn't regular size, that big kind with its own handle.

"I've been watching for something like this," Bob said.

"Anyway, maybe you should leave for a while, at least get away from each other."

I didn't know what else to do. I shook his hand and he smirked, knew he had done well. I went back and planned on reading for the next few hours. Hopefully Mark would go off to sleep somewhere.

I was still in shock by what almost happened. He nearly brained me and I never saw it. Bobby probably saved my life, kept me from the veggie patch anyhow. The bottle of thick glass, sturdy enough to need its own handle. If Mark would have hit me in the head with that jug at full swing I saw my mind going black and that enduring voice going all the way out.

Bobby came back to tell me Mark had gone out, went to his girlfriend's house. My hands behind my head, I sighed then closed my eyes.

I heard the front door open and close. Someone was down the hall.

Colin stepped in.

"I might know where my money went."

"Me too."

"You tired, Joss, you alright?"

"I'm okay."

"What happened?"

I looked at him.

"So where do you think it went?"

"I looked for that friend of his I know, said Mark's been spending like crazy, and his girlfriend."

"He doesn't feel good about it anymore!"

"What?"

He sat down at my desk.

I told the story of what took place in the kitchen. When I was finished he looked at me from far off.

"How about that?"

"Huh, glad you're alright."

He rose.

"Sorry about all this," he said.

Bobby who had kept silent looked at us now.

Mark did return, even more drunk, wasn't going to let it go, not going to stop until he convinced someone of his view. He spoke with great conviction. No one wanted to listen. I couldn't imagine being him.

The police arrived near midnight, our loud voices were scaring the neighbors.

"We don't wanna come here again," one of the cops said. "If we come here again we'll be taking you with us."

"So keep it down. Everyone try to relax," the other cop said. "Get some sleep."

The one who just spoke looked at Mark and me. The cops kind of smiled then casually backed out the door. They understood to face us as they went.

In five minutes Mark started again. Because I hit him it wasn't over. He was out of his mind, drunk and fixated. His hair ragged with moisture, eyes popping, crazed with white liquor. Spit from his lips sprinkled the light.

Bobby couldn't listen anymore, left for a friend's house to sleep. Colin went into his room and shut the door. I also went in my room.

Mark continued, mumbled, yelled with himself in the kitchen, called out, taunting mostly me.

I listened for about thirty minutes. I went out, asked him to stop. His punched me in the face. I struck him under the chin. His teeth clicked. He rushed me now. We slammed into the counter and I deflected most of the blows but got free by tagging his cheek.

He was so drunk nothing had much effect, still coming on with a stagger. As he got ready to swing I plunged a fist into his abdomen. The surprised look, doubled over and then fell down.

He didn't look at me. I left him there, got some water, went into my room closing the door.

Colin never stirred.

As my eyes were flickering asleep there was a knock on my door.

"Yeah."

I sat up.

The door opened fully.

"Are you Joss Carlsson?"

The voice was friendly but firm.

"Yeah. Who's that?"

"Police. We had another call."

My eyes had to adjust. A silhouette in the doorway was all I saw.

"You'll have to come with us."

His face still indiscernible.

"That's all right, everything's all right. I was sleeping."

"I told you if we came here again you'd be coming with us. That guy is really beat up."

I was hoping he wouldn't get insistent.

"What's he saying? He wants to press charges? Whatever's wrong with him he did it all himself."

"I don't think so, now let's go."

"He brought it on himself, don't you see that?"

"Come on."

Motioning with his arm now.

"The guy's a drunk. He did this all himself."

Strange talking with someone whose face I couldn't see.

"He wouldn't listen, we gave him a chance."

"So you hurt him."

"No, just the opposite. I was defending myself against his insane behavior. If I didn't he was gonna destroy the place."

"So, you were attempting to prevent him from destroying the contents of the house?"

"Yes, sir."

"Come with us till we can get it straight."

"Is that really necessary? I'm sleeping."

"I don't want you here now anyway."

I was wearing cut off purple sweats and a white t-shirt for bed.

"You wanna change into something else before we go?"

"No."

He looked at me queerly.

"Last time."

I shook my head.

He still had that look.

"Turn and place your palms on the wall."

I did.

"Now with your feet apart."

He searched me in my bedclothes for I don't know what. Never turn your back, I remembered. Take no chances. You imagine it and now it was happening. The handcuffs felt worse than I would have guessed, too. Nothing like the plastic sets my friends and I played with as kids.

The cop put a hand on my shoulder and faced me down the hall. I went slowly in front of him to the kitchen with his guiding hand on me all the way. We joined his partner who was standing over a sad looking Mark.

"This one going to be okay?"

He jerked his head toward Mark who was sitting at the table.

"He'll be fine. Couple bruises," the other cop answered.

"Do you think he needs a doctor?"

"You need to go to the hospital, son?"

"No."

They were convinced he was the victim, dried blood on his neck and clothing. His cheek was bruised.

I rolled my eyes and would have gone after him again if those handcuffs had been plastic. Amazing how amiable and lucid he had now become.

"We're taking this one for the night."

My cop squeezed my shoulder.

"Just call us if you still want to press charges," the other cop said.

"I will, thank you, officers."

I couldn't believe what I was hearing. Come on, Mark, put a little more sincerity into that sappy forlorn guise! Bastard! I was wrong. It was then I abhorred him most. I would have him on a burred spike sometime soon.

I was escorted to the door. The other cop opened it to the night air. I didn't look at Mark but knew he was watching me.

Outwitted by a stupid head. Shit! I hoped it was not going to be a life long trend. I was furious with myself. I just lay in bed while he set it all up.

I was marched down the stairs in my new bracelets, shoeless, wearing my sleepy time shorts and a white undershirt. The patrol car was waiting directly in front of the breezeway. I was not going to dress up for jail. It seemed more like a place in my mind instead of a real destination.

The other cop opened a rear door while his partner slid me onto the cool seat. The door shut. I was in the car by myself. It was the first hard feeling of many I would have that night. This one a sort of lonesome helplessness. I stared through the wire mesh that divided the back and the front. There were no handles to open either rear door.

I squirmed around on the slippery seat while the policemen talked quietly outside. And then to someone else over a two way.

The idea of what was happening penetrated deeper. The helplessness making me into a dependant. Part of me wanted to laugh at my predicament. Honestly laugh. Then the facts dawn on you. They are gray in color. When you see them there is no question as to what they are. They don't negotiate. They are not edgy but blunt and immovable. Where I was going was very blunt and immovable. This was the truth I was contending with alone in the back seat of the cruiser. Where I was going and what I could expect. Worse, my fidgeting triggered the cuffs to automatically tighten. I tried not to be so aware of the discomfort. It was just such a surprise.

Both cops got in the car. Neither of them said anything to me, not associating with the prisoner.

"Are the cuffs supposed to be this tight?"

"Yeah, don't move around or they'll tighten up," the one set to drive said.

"They're pretty tight now."

They mumbled back and forth.

"Don't move around. You don't want them to get too tight," the other one said.

They wore impartial little smiles. I sat back, tried again not thinking about it.

As we left the parking lot I could see many of the neighbors' faces in their windows.

Never saw Colin.

The drive to jail took us over the river. No one really spoke on the way. The one not driving answered the radio a couple of times. Once there, one of them opened the door while the other stood by. I was guided out then with one on each arm they escorted me inside.

The handcuffs were taken off and I was placed in a windowless room with two other men. Each man sat silently on a bench against opposing walls hunched over with his face in his hands gazing toward the floor. They were still and continued to look downward as I stood before them. I sat on the bench to my left. They were still motionless.

After what seemed about an hour the door swung open and I was motioned to come forward. I met the cop at the door where he took hold of my arm, brought me into what would be the processing room. Two of them had me stand up and sit down any number of times at different writing stations throughout the bright room while they logged my personal information and fingerprinted me. The tips of ten fingers smudged by their ink.

When they were finished doing the paperwork one of them handed me the jumpsuit. Crisp and clean. I was told to remove my clothes and give them over then to put on the required fashion. I put on the oversized get up then walked with a cop behind me down a narrow corridor lined with cells in what felt like the rear of the building. He ordered me to stop near the end and face right. When I stood facing the cell its door slid open mechanically revealing four bunks, three of which were taken.

I entered the cell and stood there till the bars eased shut. I then climbed into the unoccupied top bunk. My luck getting the preferred bottom bunk hadn't even held.

I tucked my hands under my head and stared at the ceiling inches from my nose while I heard them snore and mumble in their sleep. Who the hell those men were and what they had done to get themselves there kept me awake the rest of the short night. I may have slept a bit.

All three began to stir early. They sprang to life easily and spoke with one another as if they were old friends. I imagined that you got to know each other quick between the walls.

I rolled onto my side and put my head over the edge of the bunk to get a look at my cellmates. The first one who met my gaze seemed like he was waiting for me and quickly offered to let me smoke some of what appeared to be a homemade cigarette. He held it out, his first gesture to me. His eyes looked kind and weary. A thousand years in the past a ways to see from.

I shook my head.

I would have loved a cigarette, his looked suspicious. He nodded slowly, kept on twisting it.

The second man I saw was applying a tattoo to the left shoulder of the third. They were all three seated in folding chairs along the opposite wall about five feet away. There was a narrow open closet between the one smoking and the others. It was really a tall wood cabinet built off the wall. The man giving the tattoo asked if I would like one for myself. I don't think I even responded. He went back to his work without a thought.

I can no longer see their faces; I do recall the one with the cigarette and the one who offered me the tattoo were middle aged. The one getting the tattoo was younger, not a kid, had dark hair. At no time did he wince from the surgery.

The tattoo artist looked up to ask where the other had found the tobacco.

"It's toothpaste," he replied.

"Toothpaste…" the artist said over.

"Yeah, dried toothpaste. I rolled it in toilet paper."

"Any good?" asked the third man. Blood was streaming down his arm shiny in the light.

"Helluva good buzz. Keeps mah breath fresh, too."

He grinned ugly at them, almost charming. It unnerved me in that place. That you could get used to it. The others admired him for his resourcefulness then both looked away and continued with what they had been doing.

It was sun up.

I watched the man giving the tattoo, his hands working on the other man's skin. I looked carefully, in close, concentrating. He was using the blue ink from a ball point pen and a bent paper clip to scratch the design. He sensed I was watching and asked again if I would like a design for myself. No charge.

"Girlfriend won't like it."

They laughed intensely, more like cackling at my reply. I realized I spoke of a female and of life outside very casually. In too familiar a way. Had to be the reason they laughed as they did. Masking the pain that came up when they were reminded of what they could not enjoy and missed. It must be a great longing shoved away. But that each understood. My heart going out as I watched their morning. I think I was one of them.

The first shift appeared outside pushing a cart with coffee, milk and donuts. The men greeted him warmly and he replied the same. The door to our cell slid open and everyone came out for breakfast. I watched from the top bunk as they gathered around the cart. Then I think out of boredom I threw my legs over the side of the squeaky bed and hopped to the ground. I found one last dry donut and a warm cup of milk.

Taking their coffee with them the men settled back into the cell where they could sit down. The one with the new tattoo asked how long I was in for. I told him I should be getting out at noon. He looked at the other men coldly, announced he was eligible for parole in ten years, sounded like he already served five.

I climbed onto my bunk while he went on to tell us a story. He looked at each man, said he was only in the facility temporarily because of a transfer.

"What did you do?" someone asked.

His face turned sallow.

"Robbery. Bank robbery."

♠

I felt a twinge, more curious and amazed. I rolled onto my back and became lost in thought. I wondered what time it was.

I overheard the other men describing the reasons for their incarceration, discovered they were put in for lesser wrongs.

I kept to myself, stayed away from them. I thought about how he spoke of his decade long incarceration so plainly. I would be released back into the world in a few hours while he would remain there coloring his skin and eating stale donuts for ten more years. Seemed strange to consider freedom that way before then. Maybe because I enjoyed so much of it without ever thinking to worry if I would have it always.

The morning inched past, I was able to doze through most of it. When the cop came at noon he found me standing there.

"You Carlsson?"

"Yeah."

I went down the corridor.

He showed me the empty holding cell, this time the door was left open. He returned in a moment with the wire basket and my clothes. He offered me my balled up shirt and shorts looking at me curiously.

"Is that it?"

I nodded.

"No shoes? Do you have shoes?"

"Didn't come with any."

He laughed.

"Get dressed and come outside."

I changed out of the jumpsuit and into my wrinkled clothes then presented myself out front where two of them stood talking.

"Is there anything else?"

"Nope."

It seemed they had been talking about something personal, were lighthearted.

"We can call a ride for you," the woman cop offered.

"That's all right."

"You sure, it's quite a walk."

"Nah."

"Do what you want."

I obviously amused her.

I went through the revolving door to another overcast afternoon. I stopped at the curb, turned my face to the sky. I was happy to see the sky. Warm water was coming down. I had to look around to get my bearings.

Colin, still in bed. Bobby wasn't around, Mark either. I went into my room.

Nasty dream.

One hundred and forty bucks to Mark not to file charges.

It was great to hear my mother's voice.

"Hi, there. It's me. How is everything?"

"Fine, everything's good, mom. How are you doing?"

"Oh, fine."

"Well, I have some news. I think we can do something about the money. Keith said he would help you."

"Really?"

"Uh huh."

"Okay."

"I think so, yes. Just be sure you thank him. He's doing you a favor so tell him thanks."

"I will."

"Okay. Just be sure to."

"Yes, I will. Of course."

"Alright."

A pause.

"Keith wants to see you. We'd like to come down. You know, he wants to do it in person."

"Okay."

"Do you have any plans next weekend?"

"Not really. So you're coming?"

"Why don't you plan on us on Saturday morning? About eleven thirty."

No about, about it.

"I'll be here."

"What else have you been doing?"

"Nothing really."

"Work hard, Joss."

"I will, mom."

"Okay."

It was like her to pester me then withdraw a little sheepish.

"So are you buying a car, or what do you think?"

"I think a car, maybe something else."

"Oh. Well, you know to be careful. But you cannot tell Keith. If it's a car, fine, not otherwise."

"Okay."

"Alright."

My mother had a deceitful streak, more malicious than mine. It was fun to have her go along on a charade, unnerving also. Your own pretty mother shouldn't be that sly. I think I would have preferred her to be more forthright. It didn't seem her usual approach.

"Okay, Joss, I've got to go, and remember we will be there on Saturday at about lunchtime."

"Yep, no problem. I'll be waiting."

"Love you."

"Love you, too."

♣

My mother knew what I wanted but wouldn't care to go over it. It was that aspect of her I knew I could count on. Now I had something to look forward to. Other concerns went to the background.

I'd go to the dealer in the meantime with some money, they could hold the bike, maybe have it ready a certain day if I asked. Big Mike would get to work on it if he knew when I was coming back.

I went in to town across the river on the bus again to Big Mike's. Old women liked to smile at me; I stood in the aisle waiting for the door to open. Her body bobbed back and forth with the others. The driver braked, I braced myself for the swing to the curb.

Still had to walk a ways, no rain that day, wind. It blew and blew then the real heat would come, usually May.

Be good to possess a machine instead that could outrun the weather.

"Do you need any help?"

I didn't hear her come up.

"Yeah, hi. Would you be able to hold this, about ten days? Would that be possible?"

"We can do that."

"Good."

"What will you put down today?"

"How much?"

"Something, though."

"How about five hundred?"

"We can hold it for ten days with that."

Her expression went from placid to busy.

"Could you wait here?"

I'd never owned a motorcycle like this one, only ridden ones close, with Mitch, mostly, stepbrother a couple times. When I was younger I rode a lotta dirt. Nothing like what I was looking at, thought how remarkable it was being on my own.

When she returned I was in the saddle, balanced the weight between my legs so I could reach into my pocket. Handed her five undamaged green and white slips of paper.

"Next weekend okay?"

"Be fine."

"If there's a problem call me."

She nodded as she wrote.

"There won't be a problem."

She finished, handed a copy over.

"Thanks."

"Thank you."

I arrived home late after doing some studying to find Colin stretched out on the sofa. The television on in front him. When I shut the door he sat up.

"Must've been sleeping."

I could tell he'd been at it soundly.

"Where've you been?"

"Studying."

His thick hair an uncharacteristic mess. He lowered himself down to his elbows, all the way now.

I sat by his feet.

"Can hardly keep my eyes open."

He stood.

"If you want, there's half a joint in the ashtray."

"Goodnight."

"Turn off the lights, okay?" I asked.

My legs on the coffee table, watching the television, I would glance at the ashtray. Reached finally for the joint, rolled tight, a good half remained. I was too comfortable to sit up so I drug the lighter within reach using my heel. There was the acrid smell of a fire put out, the yet unlit joint up in my mouth. Didn't care it was used, the little flame bounced with the puffs. I held it between my fingers like a cigarette, rested that hand on the sofa arm. Nice to smoke it like a cigarette, no worry to share. I stood up to turn off the TV, put on music, picked a tape from a box full of them and went back to the sofa. I leaned my head back, folded my hands across my belly to dream. I loved the remoteness of the night.

"How did you sleep?"

"Really well."

I was still in bed.

"Why are you in here?"

Diana poked her head in behind him and laughed and laughed then was gone.

I grunted.

"What's wrong with you?"

I heard Diana laugh some more.

Colin was looking at me curiously. He was coming closer, held a cigarette.

"Oh, leave me alone."

He came on till he was next to the bed, hovering exactly above me.

"What do you want?"

"You're not okay."

"Huh?"

"Life outside is difficult."

"Oh, fuck you!"

"You miss living with those men?"

"Shit."

"I'm sure."

Colin had the manner of a shrink, supposing like one, held his cigarette just so.

"Do you want to talk?"

"Lean in."

He fell into the chair at my desk. He was smiling, held up the cigarette. Diana came back in and looked at me with shiny eyes.

"Wide awake you guys."

I sat against the wall.

"It's a beautiful day."

I nodded warmly.

He blew smoke.

Diana moved next to him.

"Have plans?"

"We're going out, won't be back for a long time."

He was one up.

"We're going to my Dad's house," Diana said. "He's going to make us dinner."

Colin looked at me, squeezed Diana.

"Well, that should be fun."

Neither of them said anything, pleasant looks.

"Have a good time."

The phone rang.

He was pissed but got up to answer it in his room.

Diana took his seat.

"Were you sleeping?"

"I don't care."

"Sorry about all that happened, it must have been really bad."

"I earned some of it, but thanks."

What a restful place her gaze was.

"He never got his money back. Well, a little bit. Mark spent most of it."

She obviously knew.

"Why do you think he took it?"

"I don't know, just stole it."

She just couldn't believe it.

"I gave him a little, until he starts working."

I nodded, wondered where she was going then thought that maybe she just wanted to talk.

"He'll be fine."

"Yeah, I know."

She was looking down.

"Amy was nice, wasn't she?"

"Yeah."

She hoped for more.

"Did you like her?"

"Yeah, she was great."

I smiled.

"I know she's your friend."

"I couldn't give you up, anyway."

Colin came back and now seemed impatient. He looked at the two of us and lit a cigarette. Diana looked up at him confidently. I don't remember Colin being jealous for a second in those days.

"I can wake you up every morning like this if you want."

"Like this is fine."

"We have to go soon, Colin."

"We'll go."

"Do you wanna stop or do you want me to make something to eat for the drive?" she asked.

"You can see what we have."

"All right."

She went out.

"Do you feel like anything?" she called from the hall.

"Whatever you think."

We heard her searching.

"What are you doing today?" he asked.

"Some work, I guess."

I didn't mention anything about the motorcycle. I preferred the surprise.

Colin went out, I rolled from bed, and he was right, it was a beautiful day. I showered and got dressed while they were both getting going in the kitchen.

"Have everything?" Colin asked Diana.

She didn't look sure.

"Yeah, I think so."

"Well, have a good day," Colin said.

"I will, you too."

"Bye," said Diana.

Her arms were full.

When my mother arrived that next weekend and actually walked through the door my excitement betrayed me. About a year had passed since I had seen her. She looked the same. Outwardly she was a charming and confident lady who rarely removed her sunglasses until she was well into the meeting.

"It's so good to see you, Joss."

We hugged for a moment and I felt like I was home again.

"Where's Keith?"

"Oh, he's somewhere behind me. You'd better go and help him bring some of those things up."

Just then I saw Keith through the open door coming up the stairs carrying two large sacks. It wasn't that hot of a day yet, warmer in the stairwell out of the breeze.

"Come in, mom, while I help."

It felt awkward attempting to be gracious in so humble a space.

Keith was a reliable man who had resigned himself to doing just about anything my mother asked. I believe his first marriage was an extraordinary failure. I say this based only on what I gathered from hearsay in the past. He had a pretty good sense of humor and I thought later that he had sort of retrained himself to try and avoid the pitfalls of inflexibility that undid him before. He kept up phone relations with his two children but rarely saw them. Something was bad between him and his ex-wife which I never discovered, kept him away from them so he just called. He didn't seem to mind. If it bothered him it didn't show. No aura of defeat came through.

"Let me take those," I told him.

He gratefully handed over the bags then stood for a moment at the top of the stairs.

"How are you, Keith?"

"Fine, Joss, how are you?"

"Good."

"Your mother has a carload of things."

"I'll put these inside and be right down."

"Appreciate it."

I went into the kitchen and hurriedly placed the sacks of groceries on the counter. I could see my mother down the hall, eyeballing the premises. She had walked the length of the apartment and now stood outside the door of my bedroom looking in.

"Is this your room, Joss?"

"Yeah, mom."

"It's big. Clean, too. Did you clean it for the first time because you knew I was coming?"

"No, had to be the second or third."

"Mmm Hmm."

That familiar sound in her throat.

"I'm sure."

"I'll go help Keith then we can talk or go have lunch."

"Thank you, Joss."

I remembered now how she appreciated small acts of kindness. It was nice having someone to appreciate them and say so. I ran down the stairs to catch Keith before he unloaded everything. When I walked up beside him he immediately transferred the two sacks he had over to me.

"All this going up?"

"I can't believe it either."

I went back up clutching a sack in each arm.

My mother was busy unpacking the first two bags on the counter. I set the two new ones nearby.

"Where do you want me to put everything?"

"Anywhere is fine, mom. Thanks for doing all this. This should hold me till the end of the year."

"That's what I was hoping."

She reached deep into one of the bags.

"Where are your roommates?"

"Out, I guess."

"Oh, I see."

"What?"

"Having your mother here scared them off."

"That's not it."

She didn't believe me, kept unpacking.

"Colin has a girlfriend. The other guys are just out."

"Where is Colin?"

"He's with his girlfriend."

"Girlfriend…"

A pause.

"What about you?"

"They'll never catch me, mom."

"Okay."

She smiled into a grocery bag. I didn't expect the kind of girl I liked would ever pass inspection. Without experiencing it I knew.

"Where do you want these?" Keith asked behind us.

"Just put them there," my mother said.

She was pointing to the floor by the cabinet. He leaned over to put down the bags and grunted as he made himself upright. My mother looked at him and shook her head then glanced at me laughing so he wouldn't hear.

Keith had his hands on his hips. His skin was red and white. Moisture ran from his sideburns.

"Are you two enjoying yourselves?"

I'd disappeared on him.

On the asphalt below the bumper were six more sacks. I scooped up two and went up the stairs. Keith was talking to my mother and when I approached their conversation ended.

"How many more?" he asked.

"I'll get em."

"I appreciate that."

He did seem grateful.

I saw Carrie coming out of her apartment on the first floor.

"Hi, Joss," she said locking the door. I said hello and she was beside me for a second then went another way.

I carried up two more bags. My mother was busy unpacking. Keith folded sacks, unpacked a little as they made jokes. He went slow, didn't know where to put anything where my mother was going fast telling him to just fold the sacks.

Mostly sunny that afternoon, looked forward to enjoying it, clouds high and feathery. I could feel the warm sun under the spring's pale sky, just off its peak. A light breeze, gray outline of my shadow on the pavement as I bent over to pick up the last sacks.

When I came in they had their backs to the counter, leaning on their hands, talking.

"That's it."

My mother finished making her point to Keith, began to unload the two new sacks nodding her head while he spoke.

"Is that it, Joss?" she asked turning away from him.

"No, no more."

"Make sure this lasts you."

"I know it will, thank you."

Keith went to sit on the sofa, looked around. He sipped at iced tea that I guess he made. An undissolved pile of sugar coated the bottom of the glass, a lot also suspended in the solution close to the bottom. She motioned his direction with her head so I sat down opposite him while she finished what she was doing.

"You doing alright?" I asked.

"Yeah."

I slid open the glass door, breeze came through the screen. Now we heard traffic. Someone was talking loudly in the hall downstairs, Keith sipped his tea, ice chinked when he lowered the glass.

"We have been going nonstop for two days," he began. "Shopping and packing, getting things loaded, driving, you know."

He talked like he might to someone who worked for him. He sipped his tea as he rested and glanced outside.

"I appreciate what you've done," I told him.

"No problem."

He dropped a piece of ice in his mouth.

"How about you?" he asked.

He was still chewing.

"Yeah, everything is fine."

He nodded, dug for more ice.

"Did you have fun in school?" I asked.

"I liked it."

"Did you graduate?"

"Yep."

"What in?"

"Chemistry."

"Was that your first choice?"

"Huh, not exactly."

"What did you do?"

"The army."

"Did you like that?"

"Um, yeah, I liked it."

"What did you do when you were in the army?"

"I worked on the big guns."

"Really?"

"Repairing artillery."

"Wow."

My mother was now in the living room listening to us holding her own glass of tea. Hers had good color with nothing undissolved. She sat down on the other end of the sofa from Keith.

"Well, do you have any plans for the afternoon?" she asked me.

"Only with you."

"Good. Let's have lunch, look around."

"Sure."

"Do you know a place?"

"There's a lotta places. Why don't we drive around, you can pick?"

"Okay. It's a good idea."

Keith nodded chewing ice.

We sat in the junk furnished living room talking and drinking iced tea. She and I talked mostly while Keith listened or stared outside. I watched them in the unfamiliar surroundings. Their character and fashionable clothes made them out of place.

"How much do you pay?" she asked.

"Two hundred."

"That's not bad. It's nice."

She looked around, sipped her tea.

Keith was bored. He swirled the ice in the otherwise empty glass. He had stared outside long enough, found nothing. When I looked at him he was leaning his head back to chomp more ice.

"Are you ready?" I asked.

"Sure. Let's eat," said Keith.

"Keith can always eat," she said and laughed. "Can you tell?"

Keith ignored her. It wasn't the first time he'd heard it. He stood and stretched his arms in front of him. My mother checked her face and lips.

"Ready?" I said by the door.

I told Keith what roads to take; we circled seeing a lot my mother would comment on. When we were more hungry we chose a place to eat.

We walked silently, no one used to being together. She loved pizza, spotted this place down in a basement. Since it was below decks it immediately smelled confined.

"But don't dives have the best food?" she said.

She asked what sounded good, repeated it to Keith. He ordered and volunteered to wait at the counter. We found a table, ended up at a booth in the middle.

"I love this kinda place," she said. "Have you eaten here before?"

"Many times."

"Is it good?"

"Very good."

"See," she said.

A few seconds passed.

"Do you like it here, Joss?"

"Yeah."

"Good."

"Where's Aaron?"

"He's staying with his friend."

"Didn't he wanna come?"

"He's with his friend."

"Is he doing all right?"

"He's doing fine."

"I wish he would have come."

Nothing.

"I'm going to graduate school," she said.

"Really?"

"Yes."

"That's wonderful."

"Yes."

"What made you decide this?"

"I've always wanted to."

"I didn't know."

She was beaming.

"I start this summer."

"It'll be good for you."

"I'm excited."

"I would be."

"I'll earn more at work, too."

"Even better."

"Yeah, I'm excited."

"Very good"

"Thank you," she said.

Keith appeared next to the table.

"It's gonna be about fifteen minutes."

He wasn't happy about waiting.

"No hurry," she told him. "Sit down and relax."

She slid over so he could sit down.

He was directly in front of me sipping some water. He leaned back and looked at me.

"Do you need some money?"

"I was hoping."

"What amount?"

"About three thousand."

"I can give you two."

"Two?"

"Okay?"

"Two will be fine."

And it was done. He wasn't going to move on the total. Keith looked at the table and played with the car keys. He seemed pleased to have helped. My mother looked at him then at me.

"Thanks," I said.

Keith wore a slight smile as he clicked the keys.

A girl called his name. When he came back he placed the pie in the center. My mother cut the pieces apart.

"Take a piece," she said.

It felt too good being together, part of something for the afternoon, think they also enjoyed it. We talked lightly as we ate, still nice hearing our voices at once. Going out my stomach was very full, walking more slowly.

"Did you like the food?" I asked.

"I'm glad we came," she said.

"What about you, Keith?"

"Oh, he likes anything."

Keith nodded, toothpick sticking from his mouth.

We were near shopping. Pedestrians, traffic just everywhere. She looked in store windows, we moved with people up and down the walks. My mother saw places she liked and would go inside while we waited for her. I wondered if Keith liked the girls stepping past us. All the activity he wasn't used to but seemed to be withstanding it anyway.

"It's five, Keith, we don't wanna leave too late."

She was carrying a couple bags.

"We just got here."

"I can drive most of the way home."

He made a face but knew not to argue.

"We had a nice afternoon, Joss," she told me.

"Thanks, mom, I did too."

I wasn't ready for them to leave. Keith smiling vaguely. The wind abated, chilling off ahead of evening.

We were circling closer to the car but my mother couldn't resist and went inside one or two more shops. While Keith and I waited I wanted to say how it felt not having much for a family. That having a full heart then nothing but empty is how murderers are made. I wanted to tell him how the devil was sewn to the back of my skin.

The car now in the shade, we drove away. I sat in back with my mother's bags. She bought some things but I didn't ask what they were. Keith didn't either. I don't think I cared. I only had a moment with them and didn't want to hear about shopping.

In the car in my lot we talked about people from the past, family members she wasn't in contact with anymore. *Whatever happened to him or her? How much are they making?* She liked to speculate, had some system to measure. Falling short meant she could stay away without worry, was justified. I knew she liked to be far away. I had caught on.

She liked one day trips, little time for much to escalate. It was better for her not to endure bad talk. Memories could launch it and the huge anxiety. This was her most aggravating quality. She avoided envisioning the past and was hungry to. But it was dry wood in water. This was a repelling truth for her that emptied her.

So she stayed that way, always empty.

I could not imagine not having her in my life.

So you hold on, waiting for change.

The speech was winding down and we had unbecomingly lain bare enough of the relatives. My father was a fun target for her. I didn't like it because it was also at my expense. She seemed not to be aware and we only had one day so I wouldn't spoil it.

"Well, we will see you this summer," she said.

Keith handed me a check.

"Thank you."

"You're welcome."

He started the engine.

"Do you know how to get out of here?" I asked.

"Oh, yeah, no problem."

He and I shook hands over the seat.

My mother got out to meet me and kissed me.

I was sad to see them go.

I waved and watched them drive away.

I felt drained.

Colin was leaning against the counter eating, reading a tourist magazine of the South.

"Vacation?"

"Maybe this summer."

"Did you have a good day with them?"

"Yeah, we had a nice day, good to see them."

"Did they bring all this food?"

I raised my brow.

He soon tossed aside the magazine.

"I'm going to Diana's so I'll see you tomorrow."

"Have a good night."

He was already going for the door.

"You too."

Alone with a half eaten bag of chips.

I put on some music, sat on the sofa, thought about my mother and Keith driving three hundred miles to their destination. Thought about the food, how much I would actually get to eat, remembered the dealership, closed on Sunday.

The interior of the bank an unaroused environment which put me at ease, sanctuary of privacy, safety apart from events outside. I gave the teller the check, asked her to confirm the account balance. She did so jubilantly even though it was Monday morning. She wrote my balance down on scrap, pushed it to me then held the check examining both sides.

"Do you want to deposit this?"

"Yes."

"You won't be able to access the funds until the check clears."

I looked at her.

"It's an out of state check. Count on five days."

"Five days?"

"Roughly."

The day overcast, light temperature. I went to the restaurant where Leigh and I had been. I don't remember the name, savory food at a discount. I ate breakfast in a booth by the window so I could see out.

Traffic slowed, a worried dog circled in the road. He made it over but drivers farther back were raving, horns, couldn't see the reason. I felt for my checkbook, being extra sure, afraid it got left.

"Get you anything?"

"No, thanks."

She wiped her hands with a damp towel, rolled it into her uniform pocket.

I paid and left.

I stayed close to the building. The cab pulled up, knew who I was.

"Where are you going?"

"Tenth and Meeter."

We merged with traffic, down hill for the river. On the bridge I looked at the café con leche below and watched it slide around the brushy islands in the middle. The arched bridge dropped us in the center of town where the driver made some hasty turns before coming to a stop. He had a look of desperation like we might not have gotten there in time.

"Six bucks my friend."

I let out a laugh.

The chime on the door sounded inside the showroom and the woman I worked with before appeared from behind a display, asked if she could help.

"It's over here. We don't have a lot of room in back so I found a place."

I excitedly followed, preferred dealing with her not the owner. She was plain looking but kind, thought she might be the owner's daughter.

There she was. She looked noble. Spirit made of metal. Sleek, fast, already carrying me away. A machine insinuated like a living being. I breathed a sigh. Everything would be all right. If I could stay alive while I figured her out everything would be okay.

The woman watched a few paces away. She had a mild amazed look. But my reaction had to be something she had seen before. I wondered if she was comparing how she would be or if the opposite sex just halted her with its weird mystery.

"I'll be right back."

She returned carrying a folder.

"Would you like to sit?"

I joined her at a desk.

"Anything to drink?"

"No, thank you."

She opened the file, separated papers.

"What did you bring with you today?"

"I'm going to pay the balance."

"Balance is eighteen hundred."

She didn't look at me, seemed to revere the amount.

"Does that include whatever fees?"

"Eighteen hundred and it's yours."

I started to write the check.

"There may be a problem."

"What's that?"

"I deposited an out of state check this morning."

She didn't seem concerned.

"The bank said five days."

"Would you like me to hold the check a couple days?"

"Could you?"

"I can do that."

"A few days."

"Sure."

All sizes and colors of paper.

"You will need those later."

I thumbed them.

"I'll be right back."

I looked across the showroom, sky clearing off. Cars zooming past, sat there with my proof of purchase.

She came up beside, handed the keys.

"Thank you," she said.

"All done?"

"That's it."

I remembered the Christmas I got everything I wanted.

Wasn't like that at all.

I went toward the bike.

"We have helmets if you're interested."

Easy then to spend more.

I looked at the motorcycle, sort of a marriage. I wouldn't ever be totally in charge, it may be the thrill.

I looked at helmets. It was hard taking my time because I wanted to go. But I wanted to get as much done then as I could. I chose a red and white helmet and paid the person who eventually appeared behind the counter.

"Don't run too hard today."

He wore a light blue mechanic shirt.

"Easy does it. Better for the engine."

I looked at him, he almost grinned before walking away.

I picked up the helmet, wadded the receipt into my pocket. The saleswoman was standing by the bike, asked if I cared for any instruction, needed to go through a checklist apparently. Sometimes I heard her, mostly her voice trailed off. When we had flipped every switch and stretched to see them and drawn our attention here and there or pointed out something else she stood up with her arms crossed to look at the bike with me on it then went in front and opened the glass double doors and waited.

I pushed with both legs, rolled toward the door, thanked her again as I went past under my own steam. She closed the doors. I sat on the bike outside facing the rushing cars. The grit and gravel from the road had collected in washes and loose piles along the curb.

After all her talking I still felt around for the kick start lever with my heel. Of course, there wasn't one, just a small red button below the right grip. I twisted the key and flipped a rocker switch to on then pushed the button with my thumb. The motor then alive, rest of the world all of a sudden dragged away. I waited and let the motor warm. I twisted the throttle to hear that sound. I twisted the throttle and wanted to hear that sound, gently. I let her warm up some more. I stuffed the papers in my jacket pocket, forgot to check the fuel level, have to do it when I stopped later. She was close to warm, sounded pleased. I liked her voice, listened for a moment sitting back in the seat. I reached for the helmet on the ground, pushed it down slowly over my head, fit snugly and would protect the vault nicely.

Others might have bought a bigger bike. It was assumed more power meant better performance. My bike was 600cc and lean. We would see about performance. A lot of power was good for straight lines. I preferred less power and lighter in the turns. I believed not having too much power was better. A quick light bike was best. Let the rider do the rest. Many were sure they needed more power but you really didn't need much more.

The motor was warm enough. I drew in the clutch and kicked the gear lever. I moved forward slowly, sliding out onto the road both feet dragging. Cars shot past too close but I was going slow. In the lane after a distance I lifted my feet, pushed in the choke some, came up to speed.

I wanted to get out of town, across the bridge, to the open. The wind and openness felt great with nothing between me and everything, seeing it all go past. The sensation was quite natural and I would be used to it again soon.

I continued down narrow streets seeing the access for the bridge ahead and opened her up a little. I took a couple green lights and the young engine whined, stubborn, resisting much speed. But the sound was perfect, bouncing against the walls, corridors, the buildings made.

Slowly the motor softened, confident, allowing the next increment of speed, she made quite a noise between tall buildings before the bridge. I steered around corners close to the high curbs in a rigid way, saw the storm drains and the tangled mess collected on their grating below the newspaper machines and the motorcycle jumped, shuddered over the creases and unevenness of the cross pavement.

I stopped at the light before the ramp which led to the bridge. The light turned green and the tense motor labored up the slope to the middle over the flat water where it rested and I could ease up. After the high part I coasted down the other side then through the shopping district riding in traffic without having to slow for mostly green lights. And the suspension was still stiff and new and the road worn out in stretches and I might be rattled as I went along.

I began west on a two lane street going away from campus on the backside to the hills and open country that were sweeping and grassy.

After miles of sky and rolling green and freshly tilled fields of dark chocolate chunks with all their rows neatly spread I scouted a clearing dotted with tall oak trees with an old barn after a dry but rutted ways of dual track. It seemed a good place to pull off.

Not too hard. Better for the engine.

The sky had given way to one fairly bright and light flew over the long waving grass as I turned down one of the sandy ruts toward the clearing of old trees with the barn.

I went far in away from the road and stood the bike beneath one of the sprawling trees. In the quiet shade I put my back against its trunk and slid down until I was sitting with my arms on my knees. I smelled the air which was sweet, satisfied like food or drink.

I rested, looked at the bike, content by the tree, warm and windy day. Big branches shot out above covering me. The leaves and long grass in the wind made a hushing sound. And the branches creaked and the grass whooshed around me in random ripples flashing blue and purple and silver.

A hazy sun poured down, crows over meat in the road. I watched keenly before I got drowsy, had to shut my eyes.

I sat up to the sound of a farmer's truck speeding along a gravel road that ran straight between the fields in the close distance. The blue pick-up ran ahead of a spinning cloud, heavy thumps from slamming holes. I watched till it turned onto the main road, accelerated and told the story of a shot manifold.

I wished I had some food, smoked a cigarette squinting at the sun.

> I danced in a little circle
> For just a little while
> All by myself,
> Wearing a little smile

The keys were poking out of the soil inside the soft imprint of matted grass my body had made. I stretched my arms, arched my back, a joint popped.

I walked over to the barn, weathered, boards were split gray. Something fled as I entered. Then something dropped. Silent, no sound from outside. I didn't think the structure had been used in some time except as home by smarter rodents. But it withstood the seasons and the wind; floor was earth only with matted straw, treads to the loft stairs all taken off, square opening above me where crumbled glass was below.

I went out, place exhaled when I did, a groan, filling in where I had been. I wasn't welcome, I'd brought time with me, no time inside that passed.

Shadows growing long. I sat on the bike, jostled it, listened for fuel, inhaling the scene again. Looking out over the field I pressed the start button. The engine startled my blood, took care of the silence. I pushed the helmet down which was too tight.

I rode slowly up the dry trail to the road, turned out, warm wind, I glanced behind me at the deep orange sun spilling over the landscape from a place at the edge. Just for me, on the skinny farm road.

Glad I wore a jacket, colder, bugs didn't care, didn't affect them as they rallied in puffs above, flew into me, assailing me.

Colin liked to ride the motorcycle.
Pleased about having transportation when he wanted.
I was the one took him around.
He didn't like to go by himself.
He wanted to sit on back, wear sunglasses and smoke.

One pair drew out all his self assuredness.

Carrie appeared more often. The bike was usually parked across the hall opposite her door. Something shiny and fast and they came around. Attention took having some money for gas.

Beautiful Carrie, said hello when I saw her but didn't believe I was meant for her. Never saw her laugh or barely smile. Took her for a ride once, was quiet on back. She went for the soap and water smelling boys, anticipating their mighty careers or birthright. I think she liked when they were indifferent toward her, above her. Still said hello when I saw her but she didn't ask for another ride.

I didn't see Mark a lot. Twice, three times before the year was out. No need for him to come around. Had everything he needed away from our building. Appreciated him staying away, admired it. Glad he wasn't around drunk. Bobby was around less and less too, he was older and starting to take his work seriously, didn't want to fall or get dragged in. I was a little younger and could hitch up the burden later on.

"What have you got?"
"Not a damn thing."
"Let's see em."
I put down the cards, he shook his head, raked the pot. Embarrassing. He should have been playing cards all along. I could have gotten him any number of games. He played with cold blood, never flouted his wins. That's how I knew he was good. Marginal players usually liked to make fun. Made

it on arrogance which usually didn't last too long. But Colin was on to something, I liked watching him play. I tried to bluff him that last hand, didn't know if he spotted it, his cards were damn good anyway. He beat me, didn't care what I was trying to do. Didn't laugh. I liked that. He didn't lecture me, make himself higher. Drug in the pot without a face. Almost worth losing to see him. How many was that? Think I'd been enjoying him win for nine hands. I decided to rest, look at my money. I was light. There wouldn't be much chance of getting any back. Not with only us playing.

I arched my back, walked around, hands on my hips thumbs forward. Colin leaned back, shuffled the cards. I sat down, leaned back too. Took a sip of warm beer. Colin wanted to play on but I couldn't. It would have been a mistake. I'd rather give him a loan. It was safer. I wasn't going to be his girlfriend anymore that night. With more players I had a chance, not alone, really, gave up that thinking. He watched to see what I would do. Knew it would be foolish for me. Wanted to finish me off. Natural. But I stayed out and he relaxed.

He kept shuffling the cards anyway. We talked, he shuffled like someone else might want to join, was ready. When Diana came over I couldn't get her seated at the table fast enough. It was not that I wanted her to play just to take his mind away. She did do that. Without knowing she started talking and took the whole thing in another direction. She was the sweet one. She talked on fresh topics, got him sidetracked. I put away the rest of my money. Colin noticed, put down the deck, paid attention to her.

"Were you playing?"

"We were, yeah."

"Do you still wanna?"

Colin mumbled his answer, so did I. Diana looked at the table and picked up the deck. She smiled at the cards, fanned them. Colin and I leaning back. She began a mild look of disappointment.

"Well, what's going on tonight, anyway?"

She was looking dangerous, for Diana. It was Saturday night, she'd dressed for it, looked the reason a man went out. I liked that bold side. I didn't think I'd seen it before. It pushed along the dormant blood. I took that benefit for free, she did it, I didn't have to give anything back. Colin was used to her, different perspective, appreciated her that way. He had something greater, enjoyed her altogether differently.

"William's having something," Colin said.

He picked up the cards, started dealing to Diana. He just wanted to deal, wasn't using money. I didn't say anything at the mention of William. Diana looked at her cards. They acted like they were playing a real game.

"Joss, what are you doing?" she asked.

"No plans, I think."

Colin threw down a card.

"Well?"

"Well what?" he said.

"Do you wanna go?" she asked.

Colin examining his cards.

"Maybe, I guess, later. I have to get ready, not gonna hurry to do it right now."

She nodded, put down her hand. Arranged it neatly in a fan. Colin slapped down his cards. She beat him. Damned if she didn't beat him. She didn't laugh, either. He was put off, but she didn't laugh. Colin collected the cards, redealt.

"Joss, what do you think?" she asked.

"Anything really."

I couldn't believe I said it because William did bother me. I imagined one of his parties would be memorable. More than a lot to see. That humored me the most, and at William's. There'd be many people, it would be all right. I thought of William as something double natured and wild.

She looked intently at her cards.

"Good then."

She had Colin again. There was no way I could stay there. Not with those two. She must always beat him so he takes it out on other people. And once more she didn't laugh or make fun. I was impressed. Colin took it well, put off, gathered the cards half heartedly.

"Why don't you two go over? I'll follow later," he said.

Diana didn't say anything, smiled shyly.

"Who's driving?" she asked.

"I can take us."

Now she was really smiling.

"It's about time you took me out on that. I was beginning to think you didn't want me to."

I grinned deviously.

"You stayin here, Col?" I asked.

"I'll find you later, that alright? I'll take Diana's car later. You guys go for a ride and I'll meet you there."

Diana didn't care, just wanted a ride.

I got up, was going to go change while they played a few more hands. He was playing harder with her than he had with me, not even for money. I could see his determination. Going to fuck it all up. Play like that you need to quit a while. He brashly lit a cigarette, put his head around all the smoke. Diana was relaxed, playing fine. Dressed well and trying dangerous.

I put on a pair of jeans, navy sweatshirt, t-shirt under, retrieved some leather work boots, lacing them up sitting on the corner of the bed. Even though the night air was mild it would be much cooler for the ride.

Diana looked a little bored. I sat in the chair, thought about making a drink but didn't. I wanted her to have one too, I had to ride. If something happened with her on back I'd have no excuse. I crossed my arms and looked at my boots. Diana glanced, knew we'd be going soon.

142

"How's it going, Col?"

"She's tough."

Diana raised her brow at me. She had been whipping him pretty good. Those two, of course, wouldn't play for money, she was still ahead of him. It was almost better than watching a money game. Put down her cards in that little fan.

"Ah ha!"

He won. Beat her with that last hand.

I wondered.

She wasn't really dressed for the motorcycle.

"You're going to freeze," I said.

She didn't reply, jumped up, went in back.

"You'll have fun," he said.

"You coming?"

"Later."

He got up, opened a beer.

"Just going to be nice to relax a while."

He took a drink, sat back down.

"Ready?" she asked.

She had her hands behind her, great big smile.

"Let's go," I said.

I started for the door.

She kissed Colin, said she would see him soon.

The engine jumped alive and blew apart the quiet. It roared in the adamant breezeway. I had to let the bike warm up and didn't like riding too much on the choke. I don't think I ran her all day till then. Diana stood on the bottom step waiting with her arms crossed. I better not hear anything about the cold. She had her hair back, ready.

I pushed out into the lot. Choke would just have to run. Diana came over. Her eyes sparkling. She put a leg over and snugged in behind. I looked to make sure her footrests were down. The air was brisk under a clear sky. Diana would be cold. We would finally be riding together so maybe she'd forget about it.

I didn't wear the helmet and I knew she wouldn't wear it because of her hair. I'd feel dumb anyway protecting my head and not hers, we got the wind.

We sat at the stop sign in front of my building. I felt her excitement through her hands on my waist. Street was dark, fairly busy, three smooth lanes allowed travel in only one direction. Squeezed the clutch, ran out first, brought the front up coming out of second. Her fingers dug for my sides, saying something behind me still holding on tight. Couldn't hear what so she put her mouth to my ear.

"I wasn't ready!"

I slowed and stopped at the next intersection. I turned to see Diana who wasn't sure yet. Her eyes were watering. The wind makes them tear all the time if they're not used to it. Her hair was all wild and she didn't know where to put her hands. She was trying to smile as she wiped her eyes.

She held my waist, leaned in, tried to stay out of the wind as much as she could while we wove our way through the chilly sloping streets between the river properties. I made a couple of wrong turns and we were too far down. I didn't want to tell her. Dampness floated in the air around the riverbank among the rows of run down houses. They looked less disheveled under darkness and sometimes we saw a glow in a window with life inside.

William's place was at the far end of all the properties before the woods. I came to a stop under a lamp in front of his building. The ride had been cold for Diana. Colder than she imagined but she couldn't have known. Wasn't best going at night, I'd have to remember to take her on a warm day to makeup. I balanced the bike so she could hop off.

"What did you think?"

"I liked it."

She liked it but was cold. Like trying to kiss while the phone's ringing. I put the keys in my pocket, brought my leg over. Muscles had to loosen from straddling the seat too hard. She hugged herself, motioned for me to hurry.

Quickly she was across the street, waited for me to catch up. We went to the third floor of his building, stood in front of 410. Diana knocked. She did seem to like the adventure of racing around in the dark.

I didn't get to knock another time before William filled the doorframe. Checking the guests personally it looked like. He saw me instead looked at Diana, smiling at her, hiding a fishhook.

"Diana how are you?"

He held out one big hand.

"Really good, thanks."

"Colin isn't here?"

"He'll be here later. This is Joss, do you know him?"

His face changed.

"We've met."

I wasn't a pretty girl. He didn't know anything about me either. I'm sure he didn't know we were coming. He was his lackadaisical self. Wanted more of Diana. She wasn't all he wished. He invited us in.

Others came up behind. William reached out, in the most delicate fashion shook a girl's hand. She, all of us, blushed. Gesture seemed absurd for what he was, her almost wanting to bend a knee.

He returned to us.

"Did you ride here?" he asked.

He was looking at the top of my head.

"We did," I said.

I laughed, my hair finished up like a pointed round brush. Diana put her hand to her head, afraid it might look like mine, loose only here and there.

He made an idle face.

"Bar's over there," he said.

He put a hand on my shoulder.

"I want you to have a good time."

He left us.

"Do you want something?" I asked her.

"Gin and tonic with lots of lime."

She walked away touching her hair.

Willie's place was big for only him, cast my eyes all over and the guests, mostly good looking girls, few males too see. Many of the girls drinking liquor, saw the stir straws in their glasses.

Diana talked with William till coming over, held out her drink for her. The ice was melting. She stirred with a finger, licked the finger. Took a sip, sighted the room.

"Good."

She stirred with the little straw.

"What an interesting guy he is," she said.

"He doesn't understand why Colin isn't here. He thinks I'm with you."

She held out her glass.

I held up a hand.

She took my sip.

We stayed in the living room about thirty minutes.

Some came dressed up. Most were casual.

"I'm going for another," I said.

"Here, thanks."

I left Diana by some girls I didn't know. Didn't know another soul.

When I returned she was gone and I searched room to room. I just didn't know anyone. Found her with some people in a back bedroom, sitting on a bed with her legs crossed. William was standing and talking. There were many beds in his house. He talked and the girls listened. There was only one other male and he looked uncomfortable and bored. I made my way over to Diana and sat on the floor with her legs hanging next to me. I gave her the drink. William motioned gracefully while he made his point, leaned over to breathe in a big line of cocaine from on top of a chest. Threw his head back, long hair flying, held out a section of straw to the blonde next to him.

The circle finished all of what had been put out so William put out more, which we finished too. Diana did a little and I could see she had done it before. Cool the way she did it. She wasn't committed to what was going on around, looked at me this one time, would have laughed if we were at home. She gulped the drink, William kept talking. He was an odd poet, moved his arms slowly, horse of a man. I saw he liked to listen to himself. No one would ever say stop. Even if he were not so princely he had much to offer for those with the longing.

Most there not the kind I'd find myself with. I didn't see something I recognized. The idea was mournful, so little to stir some interest.

He spoke to us as if we were in his classroom. I was standing up now.

"Things going your way?"

He gripped my shoulder like we were brothers.

"Where's Colin tonight?"

"He had other things to do. He'll be here later he said."

He was disappointed Colin didn't come.

"He's going to marry her you know."

He pointed discreetly to Diana.

"He probably will."

"You having a good time?"

"Yes," I said.

William put on another face turning away.

Diana still on the bed, leaning back on her arms, kicking her feet one then the other over the side making a noise with her heels against the brown metal frame. I sat next to her similarly.

"You all right?"

"Yeah, daydreaming."

I looked up at the ceiling with my arms behind me, heart smooth and the seconds racing inside themselves, kicking our legs back and forth over the side.

"Are you having fun?"

"Uh huh, this is exactly what I needed."

I know she meant a different perspective. She was on her own and didn't have to be part of something. It must have been nice to consider that sometimes. To be alone. Like having a lot of room, it's not always bad. When the room is too much is when you might want to change. Seeing everything together can be good. Guess it depended on what time it was for the one thinking about it. Diana looked out into the room, dreaming. I cannot remember anything we could have gone over. I'm sure we sat on that bed and talked for some time, which she kept with her heels. I got tired of hearing my noisy heels and had stopped. William was preaching to the girls and the one guy there. The only one except me. He looked interested and William was wound up. The guy watched the girls then stared at William. The guy was stealing a ride. William went on and was waving his arms. Horribly deliberate and animated. That with his stature, what he offered, hypnotic. I wondered what Colin saw. I thought and realized what he saw. A store and he was being nice to the owner. I'm glad he wasn't hypnotized. Those people there were entranced. My mind went clicking. Diana's made her dream. Diana, dreaming, knocking her heels on the frame.

"Your girlfriend is pretty quiet," the guy said.

He was two people over and leaned behind them to talk. I didn't hear him so much as caught sight of him lean.

"She's fine."

He nodded and leaned up.

"I'm fine," she whispered.

It was nice to hear from her. I think she stopped dreaming and was paying attention to what William was doing. He distracted her and she watched him. Some of the other girls spoke with each other but no one talked to the guy. He didn't look dejected just far away. He would have been the hardest to talk to. It would have been tiresome getting to know someone then. It would have been hard suffering small talk. So no one spoke to him.

Not a thing on the walls. I didn't know how he could have stark walls even if his stay might be temporary. All the colorlessness eating in. There was nothing to inhibit it. I made believe there was, that seemed to help, or looked away. Something on the walls gave me a place, specific. I knew I was sitting squarely on the bed. William went out, the others followed. Except the guy and one girl. She was talking with the guy. I ended up proud of him there. The girl sat between him and Diana. Diana's glass was empty, not even melted ice in it, cotton ball brushfire in a desert on the sun.

"Would you care for something?"

"Yeah, get me something would you, Joss?"

"Sure, anything?"

"Sounds okay."

I got two large glasses of ice water. William was across the room leaning against the wall as he listened to someone. When he saw me raised his glass, tilted it. Made a quick face acknowledging him before going down the hall.

We were alone when I returned.

I handed Diana the water and sat down.

She was kicking her legs.

"I'm okay now."

I knew not to question. She just didn't have any idea before. She was all right. Drank the water in fast sips.

"If you need more you tell me."

"Okay."

She drank about half then held the cup on the bed, on the wrinkled spread.

I drank as I sat with her.

She wasn't banging her heels anymore.

"Do you remember what I said to you?"

"I think so."

"Good."

She twirled a piece of her hair with an amused expression. She drank most of the water, rattled the ice.

I stood then reached out, she took my hand to pull herself up, followed me out of the bedroom. The party was still on. My eyes full wherever they went, colors warmer outside as well. It was not so stark. The walls were painted darker, pictures hanging. It made a difference after the room before. I filled our cups with a little more water and ice.

We didn't know anyone except William, went his direction. Diana started talking with some of the girls from before. If she hadn't been there I would have been gone. Her eyes on me, urging me to join. There was nothing as wild anymore and my galloping senses were running me down.

"How are you doing?"

"Alright."

"Could have used you a couple times."

"I know."

"Glad I wasn't drowning or something."

"I'd getcha."

"You'd have to admit you heard me."

"I would, quickly."

"I'm kidding. Are you doing alright?"

"Yeah. How about you?"

"Talking with those people."

"Didn't wanna say something dumb."

Laughing. "It needed to end."

I went to the bar, filled our glasses again. Enough to have something to sip on. And she was content with the water I kept bringing her. I know why I kept drinking water but she didn't have to, soothing and cold.

"Do you want anything else?"

"This is good."

"You sure?"

"Yeah, I don't want anything sweet right now and I don't like beer."

"Okay."

"What do you think?" I said.

"I don't know if Colin is coming. Did he tell you he was coming?"

"He thought maybe later. But I got the impression he would come."

"Yeah, I did too, so I don't know."

"Did you try to call him?"

"I guess I could do that."

She walked away to find a phone.

I was ready to go if Colin wasn't coming, even if he was.

Diana was a while getting back.

"This place is getting crazy!"

"Did you talk to him?"

"He said he fell asleep. Said he would come. I told him it was late. Then he said just to see him at home."

"Let's do that then."

Behind her glass I noticed she was not sure how she felt.

"You say he fell asleep?"

"That's what he said."

"That's all right."

"Yeah, tonight was our night."

She was used to Colin being there all the time and even though she might have had fun with me felt more or less abandoned.

I didn't feel let down, now could go.

I felt some joy at my friend's foolishness.

"You want anything else?"

"No. Have to find William."

I tailed.

"Is he showing you a good time?"

"Yes, he is."

"Are you going?"

"Colin is sorry he couldn't make it."

"What happened?"

"Lost track of time."

"Well, glad you could come."

"Why don't you sit with us?"

"No," Diana said.

She touched his shoulder, we were going.

Diana saw those girls again, said goodnight to each of them, talking with them for only a moment. One of the girls asked when she could have a ride on the motorcycle.

"You ready?" Diana asked me.

The air waved cool, washed and breathable. Walked next to her down the steps. Silent outside, good to be delivered from the show.

Straddled the bike, got her running. Balanced till Diana had her arms around me, laced her fingers, wasn't too shy anymore. I popped the gear, got us moving.

I took all the right streets this time. William's place wasn't hard to find but lost after a lot of short, segmented roads. Diana hung on, leaned in. So late. No traffic. Streets dark, seemed like we made too much noise as we rode.

We were stopped at a light, her face against my back, shivering.

"I can drive if you don't feel like it."

She chuckled, buried her face. Afraid my body was too cold to give her any relief other than as a shield. My eyes watery and some may have been running down. The breeze cut me but I would not have traded it. I liked going past all the shadows and dark corners as the only living vibrant thing. That other waited and I was happy to keep on. The first part of the ride was usually simpler but the way home could be long without what you were looking forward to coming.

Only the hood light on above the stove. Diana and I in the kitchen, she went back. Heard the bathroom door close.

Colin emerged from the dim hallway. I was in the front room by the glass door looking out to the street.

He lit a cigarette and came over.

"How was it?"

"What I expected, still had a great time."

"Good."

"You have a good night?"

"It was nice," he said.

I just looked at him.

He exhaled smoke.

"I liked it. She had fun?"

"I think so."

He smiled, took a drag.

"Appreciate what you did."

"Had a great time."

"That's good."

"Is she mad at me?"

I breathed a laugh.

"She might be."

He shook his head looking down.

"I think she'll be okay. Just freezing, both ways."

"You knew she would."

"Yeah."

"How did she like it?"

"I'll take her on a warm day."

"Yeah."

"She was freezing and it was dark. She wasn't dressed for it."

He took another drag.

"There you are."

He looked up at me as he put out his cigarette.

"What have you been doing?"

He gave her a big hug; she didn't know what to do. Hugged him back, nose in his hair.

"Jeez," she sighed.

Must have been after twelve when I heard him asking.

"Do you want something? Can you eat anything? I'm making breakfast, if you want anything."

Since he woke me and mentioned it I could smell the food. I turned over in bed and looked at him unblinking. He was leaning against the jamb slightly pleased he woke me.

"What?"

"I'm making something to eat, what do you want?"

"Eggs."

"Be ready in about ten."

Twelve-thirty.

Not bad.

Bobby kept a regular schedule and had become serious.

Colin and I kind of ruled the roost.

Glad he woke me.

I would have slept too late, scrapping the day resetting a new one in the morning.

I wandered toward the bathroom, smelled his cooking on the way. Made me think of a safe home. Forget how off track I was. I was able to push through the fabric inside my head. I shuffled into the kitchen and slumped down at the table. Stayed in bed clothes. Colin appeared to have showered and been dressed for some time. His hair was neat and dry. I yawned and watched him. He stood with his back to me in front of the stove, stirring. His familiar ashtray on the counter next to him. Nothing was smoldering, an odor I didn't want. He'd light one soon enough. He stirred the eggs in the pan, adjusted the burner. Couple other sides going, sautéed mushrooms, sausage rounds. Felt like I was being waited on. Suspected I was right for that kind of life, waited on by people in my home. Then the notion just struck me trite.

Colin finished up and lit a cigarette. Stirred and smoked some more. I watched to see if ash would get in the pan. Didn't see anything but his back was to me. If something did fall I wouldn't be able to tell, wind up with better flavor. I was relieved when he put the cigarette down, stopped waving it above, holding it in the same hand he was stirring with. Many who smoke find a way to do so much with it in their hand, adept at doing anything with a cigarette. Whatever he was part of usually held the aroma or was salted with specks of ash.

"This is a surprise."

Chopping.

"Thought we would eat together."

Whisking and flipping.

"Thanks for waking me up."

"It's a sunny day so I thought we'd eat and then go for a ride."

His back was still to me.

"Get a couple plates, in the dishwasher."

I stood up, pulled the plates and some silverware, gave him the dishes, forks on the table. Started to feel better as we ate.

Sat at the table and didn't want to move. It was exhausting sitting. It was mostly overcast, sun sometimes. Maybe the sun would win out. Looked like it might. The weather could go to extremes inside a single day. I'd heard before it was that way all over the Midwest. Weather never steady but extreme and capricious. It explained quite a lot. I massaged my neck. He cleaned up, went by the glass door looking at the sky.

"Are you going to be up for a ride?"

"How do I look?"

He laughed.

"I feel fine."

"You don't want to move."

"I'm okay."

Sun came through, changed to bright on him.

I turned on the shower, adjusted the water where it didn't burn my hand. Leaned against the wall under the stream, hot to penetrate my skin.

Heard Colin on the phone while I was getting dressed. Sounded like he was in his room. I found him out front when I was ready, on the ledge.

"Why don't we ever use this grill?"

I could hear him through the screen, standing over a small rusty kettle grill.

"Not mine."

"Hmm."

He turned.

"I can never hear the cars when we're inside."

I sat on the sofa, tied up my boots, leather on the toes was gouged.

He slid open the screen.

"You ready?"

I nodded.

"Let's go."

My jacket was over a chair at the table. Found the keys and my sunglasses on the counter and followed him out the door.

The motorcycle was alone under the stairs. Only spot I could find. Nice to see her there every time. In the open, easy view, breathed a little slower saw her when I came down.

I swept up the kickstand, got the motor running. Fuel was low so we'd have to stop. I knew which station. He jumped on behind and we were going. The weather mild, sun trying to come out full time. He had his sunglasses on, always started a trip looking directly at people he saw, remind them they were stuck in a car or walking.

I kept with the wind. Helmet was slick to look at, wondered why I paid two hundred dollars for it, had no appeal. If I ever decided I needed it be top shelf of the closet.

We started down the one way road in front going around some three miles to the incline before the river. At that point above, a small filling station which overcharged but was convenient. It wasn't hard getting on and off the road with fewer headaches from traffic. Colin sat on the raised concrete pump island watching cars go past. I thought he would smoke there between the pumps, he didn't. Filled the tank, went in to pay, cost little more than two soft drinks. Colin was wiping away some fuel that had spilled on the side of the tank. I tried not to but was impatient.

He held the side of the seat while he smoked, looked about as we rode below by a shopping area. I never had to remind him when to really hold on, seemed to know. Pretty nice day, river bulging and full as we went along. Big hurry and angry, trying to resolve the surplus. Large trees, high on the bank, surrounded by water. I don't think anything fascinated me more than witnessing nature. Two weeks ago the river ran low, burnt green between her banks. Today swollen heavy and muddy brown. Changes like that awed me. Stepping outdoors, like being granted new life every time. We went away from civilization, north beside the stripe of pushing, racing current.

The river a few feet away slid steadily by, could see the overflowing brown water making slow swirls above the deep spots and around exposed tree roots near the invaded, grassy shore. Trees everywhere had become well shaped, round, rich green out of the recent warmth. Ones between the road and river went in a long neat stretch, without a break. Perfect, restful shapes made to belong in place for all time.

The air dipped down, cool under the dense ceiling of high branches spread out overhead, above the water leaning out over it sometimes as the wind creaked the heavy growth and made it sway as we rode under. Colin was quiet as we ran down along through this peaking reborn landscape.

And when he saw, pointed quickly to the place where our road met another but whose entrance lay hidden behind the thick growth. I knew where the turnoff was but he remembered too, letting me know. Slowed and rounded the almost invisible left going wide to avoid the slough of loose gravel and sediment that had run off and collected.

Before the true spiral of Soldier's Town was the long ride up. Beautiful, straight through a tunnel-like canopy and reminded me of the long clanking uphill pull before the most violent section of a roller coaster. We enjoyed the scenery before the violent part. What lie ahead on the other side was like victory, anyway, if you could hold on.

Soldier's Town cut down to the river and began at the foot of a long rolling incline, led far away from the valley. The first part of the road went back in from us at a steep angle then rose quickly into the silent wooded hills.

Colin flipped away a smoke, leaned in more, gripped the edge under him with both hands. Up the steep and narrow grade, light breaking between leaves and needles. Colin aligned himself to avoid the gnats at eye level.

We sped across the summit, shifted to slow down so we could look out below. We took it in without saying anything, continued with the view fading behind the trees as we went deeper into the plateau.

The lush greenery of the hills that lead down to the valley subsided and the earth turned brown, divided up in flat squares, marked by neat, freshly tilled rows.

The narrow road curved gently at first then much more and tighter. But without a crop in the way it was easy to see ahead.

Colin checked his grip as I accelerated through the turns. We seemed to glide, rising and falling, nice rhythm with each curve. Swaying fast down and right going inside then rising up on the outside and again down and left to the inside. All in an unbroken motion, keeping the power even, letting the momentum carry us through the corners. Asphalt, mostly dry, had to watch for the occasional dirt clod kicked up by a farm tractor as it emerged from the fields to use the road as a turn around.

I saw coming up one of the few blessed straight-aways the road provided, as we went into the last curve Colin saw it too, hooked an arm around my waist as I rolled the throttle tight in my hand. We tilted out of the turn, almost snapping up like we might lift off. I loved that and the huge sensation.

He changed his hands back under him as we shot over the straight. The scrub and fields blurred away to brown wax, made us go faster and faster, water drawn from my eyes.

The straight was ending, leading to another curve, downshifted and moved forward slightly as we rode through not as antagonistically as before. Leaned through the turn and I noticed the freshly ripped apart soil extending out from the edge of the road far into the field. Gouges in the dirt as wormy cuts. Crash marks of another rider. Lost sight of the straight, slid out of the turn. May have been riding at night. Straight before was long, he didn't anticipate another curve.

But it was clear by day. Some guys out there during the night. Added to the uncertainty. I thought about Mitch who usually rode that way.

We tilted and shoved our way in and out of a new series of slow coils as we went toward the mouth of the valley. The land spilled away from us now at the end near town again. We kept going down toward the mouth.

The road opened up and straightened out as we passed above a tree line ran along the edge of the valley leading into town. We went near a small cemetery which seemed a handsome place to rest. It was in the shade with a black fence going around. Taller upright monuments leaning over all directions, sure the small plat was very old, fertile soil and crawling roots causing the shift.

"Do you feel better?" he asked.

He couldn't see me. I nodded though, rode down the grade.

"Think we should go to The Banks?"

I wanted to ride, wasn't hungry.

"I think we should go."

He lit a new cigarette. We had nothing pressing, rode to see everything. The wind was warm and the sun had prevailed and shone gold most of the day. Only threats above were wisps sketched dreamily in patches that would not rally to gray. Once we saw the sights we were ready to stop mostly because we didn't want to go home.

It used to be a bait shack resting beside the river underneath a railroad bridge. Mostly solid drinkers from town. The food was surprisingly good, portions were large and inexpensive.

We liked the cheapness and the fish. Came across the place looking for something else one time.

Colin and I pulled into the lot, parked between two of the big domestic cars that were the only kind there. He jumped off, stretched till he almost broke.

We scuffed across the chalky lot to the entrance.

"Great ride," he said.

Caught the door, ambled in behind him.

My eyes had to adjust to the bent light before I took too many steps. Most of the regulars seated at the bar paid us a tired glance, faced back taking a drink from their glasses. Thought it must have been a sight, strangers dotted with bug parts, hair all the way back, but none paid any attention. That was another reason to like the place.

"You fellas need a table?"

Auley seemed to be in charge. Quit angling for little onions, screwed the cap back on the jar. I don't think he remembered us, hesitant to make it known.

"That'd be fine."

"Sit wherever you like, someone'll be over shortly."

Colin thanked him, reached over the end of the bar to accept the menus. Audience restarted their mumble.

He put the menus under his arm, I walked behind him through the dining room looking at the walls decorated with period photographs, past events like building erections, landmarks. I recognized a couple landmarks, eyesores now. Once a lot of pride and hope in them. Pictures of the river, downtown, people gathered in front of the building outside, bar itself. Other photos, those proud in front of their cars. He stopped at a table around the corner on the far side of the room by a window overlooking the gliding water. Current sparkled with the remaining light, red and blue above the trees on the bank opposite.

We took off our jackets, tossed them next to the wall, sat down on the red vinyl inside the booth. I looked around some more before unfolding the menu.

"Unusual place," I said.

"Needs more sunlight, aired out, but what do you want, no health code violations or some mean walleye?"

His cheeks made deep red by the wind.

Other people seated, none too close. Could speak freely, not be over heard. Smoked cigarettes, talked quietly, showed their affection across the table.

The collection, many with faint eyes, reminded me of a painting I'd seen in a book. Related to a condition we didn't aspire to. Those there had the same disillusion, the unvariedness of their lives made me feel as if I needed a breath, almost too old the instant they were born.

"Get you a pillow?" he said.

"What're ya havin?"

"Walleye special."

Closed the menu, did sound good.

Waitress, leaning restlessly, waiting for us to close our menus now arrived.

"Two of your baked walleye specials please, draft beers."

Colin glanced at me to be sure.

"Is that it?"

Handed her back the folded cards.

"You seeing Diana tonight?"

"She has to work then some project at home."

"My parents will be here sometime in the next couple of weeks," he said.

"Visit?"

"Take most of my things back. Think I'll stay here with Diana till about the last day."

"Take everything?"

"No, I'll keep some clothes and whatever else I need to get by on for a few days."

"Parents coming back when you're ready to leave?"

"I'm sure they would, or Diana, or you and I could ride up together."

"Yeah?"

He pushed his glass between his fingers.

"We still have time. What about Diana, how are you gonna leave things?"

"Have it worked out, she'll travel up to see me when she can, get down here to see her when I can too."

"I don't think you will. Once you're up there for the summer nothing's going to bring you back down."

He smirked.

"The girl will do most of the driving I believe."

"Everything will be okay."

Felt as if I said too much.

He looked at me.

Turned my head to watch outside.

"What about you, when are you leaving?"

"When finals are over I'll be going back. Have to make money."

"Have anything lined up?"

"Not yet, good idea where to look."

He nodded, probably thinking about the same thing.

"How you gonna get yur things back?"

I didn't speak of my family.

"Same as you. Probably call my dad. Don't have very much."

"Does he know about the motorcycle?"

I shook my head.

"Didn't think so."

Didn't want to talk about it.

"You think it'll be a problem?"

"I don't know, been wondering."

Now he had me thinking. Old man could be pretty intolerant.

Waitress slid the plates in front of us. Skin on the fish.

Colin finished, pushed the empty plate to the edge. Touched his pockets till he felt the cigarettes and lighter. Shook one up from the pack, put it between his lips before sliding the box over.

"I like this place."

Pushed my plate to within reach, she floated away toward the kitchen with the dirty dishes. Took a cigarette from the pack. Colin gave me the lighter from his shirt pocket, smoked finishing our beers. We looked out, no daylight, river had disappeared. Smooth black, shapeless reflections here and there.

Bill came.

"I got it."

He quickly made a reach.

"You gonna leave all that?"

He didn't have to pay for everything.

Put on my jacket on the way to the door. Girl and Auley said thanks. Colin held up a hand to say it was all good.

"See you next time."

They cocked their heads at the bar to see. Few more than before.

Bike waiting in the dark. Sat down on the cold seat reversed out of the space with my legs. Put the choke on, started the engine as Colin swung a leg. We were a little down river, decided to go using another bridge. Pulled out of the lot then right going toward it. Rode under a blinking red signal toward the entrance which seemed a lesser portal.

Crescent moon rising above the trees along the shore. Man treading away from us on the catwalk, hard to apprehend in the shadow, behind the ironwork, held onto the handrail as he went over the grated footpath.

Air much cooler now, wind made my eyes fill, had to blink to see as I accelerated over the desolate span. Changed gears, sound of the engine was enormous because we were alone on the bridge, except for our man, and the night was so quiet. Lights of rentals, school came into view at the middle, engine echoed loudly between the heavy crossed black trusses. Sped across the second span, at the lights, not thinking about anything at all.

On the other side we rode through a shopping area on the south edge then up another steep incline past more shops and a big stone hotel. Number of people darting in and out of the surrounding buildings. Their forms resembled startled cats trying to decide which direction to head.

Slowly approached the breezeway. He hopped off, started going up. I shut down the engine, pushed the bike under the steps.

He left the front door open. Didn't see him, went down the hall to my room. Sat on the bed to remove my jacket, tossed it the direction of my desk chair. Hunched over and pushed back my hair. Seemed like a long time since I'd been home.

As the term drew to a close it became more important I paid closer attention to my studies. I would familiarize myself with the material enough to pass each subject. I could have let everything slide but it just would have meant starting over. It would have meant starting over and rehashing the same required material, be paying twice to go over the same course work. Also be contending with a poor academic record. I didn't wish to endure all the repetition.

As I sat in front of the glass appreciating the still I thought about money. Sun had risen, no cars going past that Friday. Silent part of the morning. I knew I had to make a trip to the insurance office. Aaron asked my father once why there had to be money at all. It was a narrow answer any landlord would've given. My brother didn't see the need. He thought we could barter for everything we required. My father told him to think about it some more. Aaron was showing promise as an artist. My father believed art was what was wrong with the world. He usually dismissed his sons' ideas quickly because of that. I couldn't tell who was right. I tended toward my brother's point of view. It seemed less exclusive, more fair and humane.

Stiff air like a slap as I rode up the sunny gray street to the early class. Those with permits occupied all the sensible parking spaces around the lecture halls. Motorcycles with no permit were also prohibited from parking in the most convenient lots despite any argument about size you could think of, so I went to a garage not far away that let me stay all day for three dollars.

At the end of the hour we were given the next week's writing assignment and there was the usual moaning and protesting. The professor went on clarifying stoically but was interrupted by more commotion as class ended.

I traipsed down the packed hall. Think I must have bumped into every person. Climbed the basement stairs to the first floor exit. Sky was cloudy, made it seem cold. Street busy with people going everywhere. I found the frenzy stimulating. They went past in their cars or on bicycles but most were walking. And so much life made me start to feel willing again.

Up the walkway to the garage. The attendant saw me; she smiled weakly from her clear box. The sound of the engine friendly and the noise bellowed in the hollow garage. I made my way to the first level going down in a clockwise spiral, ended at the gate. Paid at the booth, clear box wasn't pleased at all before raising the barrier.

The air a little warmer now. Rode through the crowded streets of the Corners, over the river into town.

Agency I was looking for was on 13th next to a law firm. Watched the shingles, riding slowly. Insurance office tucked away at the end of 13th under an awning. Inside was clean, also stale. Man and a woman sat waiting behind a counter. Guess I presumed I would have to cool off in a waiting area before escorted to the back and some unseen room.

"How may we help you?"

He stood up from his chair. I must have looked young and unwitting.

"I think I spoke to you on the phone about a policy for a new motorcycle."

He looked at the woman sitting next to him, she couldn't think. He turned back to me.

"Do you have it here with you?"

"The motorcycle?"

"Yes."

He acted like a clerk. Trained his mind to extract the details, find the remedy.

I let him have the papers I brought, placed them on the counter but before he inspected them put on his glasses.

"Let's see, what do you have?"

Sorted the papers identifying what he needed. Found just two pages that interested him before he returned to his chair.

"It will be just a few minutes."

He dictated to the woman while she typed up some kind of form.

"Address and phone number please."

I recited the information.

Comical to see the couple perform with almost theatrical seriousness.

"Are you a permanent resident of this state?"

"Yes."

"Will the motorcycle be driven by anyone other than yourself?"

"No one."

Keys kept right on clacking, man's fingers now punched buttons on an adding machine.

"How much coverage would you like?"

"Here's what you and I went over on the phone."

He and the woman did some comparing.

"We always quote a higher price over the phone."

He wished to explain, I was looking forward to a lower premium.

The woman typed looking at my notes. When she was through they both looked at me at the same time.

"Four-twenty-four," he said.

"Per year?"

"Yes, per year."

Price only a little better than before. Seemed fair though for what I was asking them to do.

"Who do I make this out to?"

"Umbrady Insurance."

His white face waited while I wrote. It was starting to feel like money well spent. Gave me something called a binder with his business card. He tucked everything into an envelope and thanked me.

Woman stood close to him.

I liked the guy who taught the next class. He was a retired broadcast journalist. It was clear how much he enjoyed working with the students. He inspired them, reveled in their achievement. He was more than casually interested in his subject. Would tell stories about his life and career and of messy situations he covered overseas. He endeared himself to us. His stories captured all of our attention. Some were quite heartrending. Been present during some of the world's most dire events. Fascinating people he knew were woven into each account. That day was no different, it was also Friday, class would be more casual than usual.

Sometimes he would try to lecture from a textbook and from notes but that was too confining and instead he would cite an example or recall a specific incident and abandon his intended format. He thought he wanted to use the book because everyone else did it that way so he kept trying but it didn't work for him. I think he was worried about his effectiveness. We leaned forward at our desks with our chins in our hands.

The hour happened quick, class over and it was time to go but many would stay. They would gather around the podium, urging him to finish the story if he had not. They only wanted him to finish and he usually indulged them. The ritual could go on for long after, many times I would have to leave before the true end.

Colin walked right in front of me on the sidewalk. Sunglasses on, had to be someplace, one hand in his pocket, other held a cigarette.

"Hey!"

"I didn't see you," he said.

I couldn't see his eyes.

"Where are you going?"

"To the bank, mail some letters."

"What are you doing?"

Walked with him at his exaggerated pace.

"Paying bills?"

"Yep. Pay everyone before I go."

"When are your parents coming?"

"Be here Sunday."

The place was busier than I thought, weather perfect to sit outside though. Greeter and I snaked our way till we reached an empty table by the rail.

Water came, tried reading over the insurance coverage. It all seemed okay in Greek.

I looked up.

"It's official," he said after sitting.

Took a drink, glass came to rest on the table harder than he intended.

"I'm outta money."

He finished the water in troubled swallows.

He looked at me with the fervent eyes of desperate person.

"I know this is funny," he said.

"It's not."

Waitress came, ignoring his statement about the blade.

"Know a game tonight," I said.

"Yeah?"

I nodded.

"Where?"

"What'd they say?"

"Well."

"Good one?"

"Should be."

I chewed some ice.

Eventually left him at the table.

I came out of my room at nine. Lots of noise from the kitchen. Said hello to Bobby, cleaning dishes, sounded like he was smashing them.

Let the hot water in the shower beat on me. Too hot but I just let it beat on me. Leaned against the wall under the flow. Came out with a big beach towel wrapped around my waist. Saw through the crack Colin's door made. Couldn't see him. But I smelled the smoke.

"You ready soon?" I said.

"I'm fine."

Turned on the radio. Bobby sat across the room talking on the telephone, nodded at me in stride with his conversation. These days he was mostly unavailable to us.

Colin came into the kitchen, knew I'd made something, pacing around wondering what it was. Began to make something of his own.

"We can go when I'm done?"

"Whenever you're ready," I said.

"What time is it?"

"I think almost ten."

Colin put his plate on the counter, began to go through unopened mail. Found his keys near the stack.

"We riding over or what?"

"Think I wanna walk."

He wasn't happy about going on foot. Shoved his cigarettes in his pocket.

Not talking a lot as we smoked. Already gone about a mile.

"Big trees."
We came upon the drive. Looked up, tremendous forked arms reaching out. Closer in light from the house showing most of the lawn. People in a mob by the door, cars all over. Didn't expect so many people, thought we'd have a game with some guys I knew from before. I hadn't been around in a while. Knew them from before when I used to see Anson more. Saw Jimmy, he wondered where I'd been, told me about the game. Would be great if I could come. Thought it would be a quiet one. Colin spiked his smoke, seemed to perk up.

"Carlsson that you?"
I remembered Kizzy.
"Good to see you."
"What's all this?"
"Big tonight."
"You seen Anson?"
"He's around."
"And Jimmy?"
"You come for Jimmy?"
"Came for a game."
"I know you'll find him."

Colin and I pushed our way inside the colossal place, always seemed inviting to me because of the tone of the wood. Finished throughout in pine, deep brown knots.

Anson might have been inside, didn't expect to see him, usually cloistered away. Went to find Jimmy, if he was playing I knew where he'd be.

Colin followed me down a creaking staircase to the basement couple levels below. Basement expansive, divided in many sections. Foundation was finished rough, walls jagged randomly. Narrow corridors took you where you needed to go. It was in them you scraped yourself. Walls were sharp. Passageways barely wide enough. Lucky to have all the light bulbs working. Couldn't believe people slept down there. Bobby would have. Not my kind of solitude. Liked sunlight too much not masonry.

The corridor we traveled emptied into a room. Exit that was really a fire door on the far side. Room was in a remote corner of the house at the base of a grade. The fire door opened to some stairs that ran beside the house going up the slope.

"Look who it is popped out our end."

Jimmy was on his feet.

"You finally made it."

"That last twenty yards."

"Use some first aid?"

Colin glanced at the back of his hand, blood running down a finger.

Three sat around a worn game table. Was just like before and not difficult catching up. The other two I'd seen. They were with Jimmy so it didn't matter. It's possible to look at a person and know that you'll each get along. I was sure they fell asleep there in that wandering tomb. Scraggy beards and wide eyes of those comfortable dwelling down below.

Scott and Leo hissed their pleasantries, liked them right away.

"Hope you brought some money with you," Scott said.

He had no idea. I'd given some to Colin so he could play.

"Put my last dollar on the plate."

"Bunch of shit."

"Guy can't buy glory."

Colin started to smoke.

"Whose deal?"

Colin cut the cards.

"Have a drink," said Leo.

"Yeah, have a drink," Scott seconded.

Scott distributed the chips we bought. Twenty apiece. That would have to do it. I could turn the conversation into more than that. That's how I enjoyed it. Let them hustle and work. I would catch a few then go over and pet the dog. I would pet the dog anyway. Odds said I would be petting the dog lighter than when I came. Poured that drink.

"Ice?"

No answer.

I sat out when my play was flat. Kept something in my pocket. I wasn't getting creamed but I was down. Didn't treat it like work just enjoyed the play. Leaned back in the chair, sipped my drink, dog came over after some goading. Colin was up but it hadn't been easy. He was unmoved. Play until it was over, till the last.

"You better dig deep if you want to catch up," Jimmy said.

"Dug a hole already."

They just wanted my money on the table. Didn't know Colin was the player. The dog and I watched things go round. Colin was still up. That last hand had everybody sighing after. They still didn't see Colin but he took their attention off me.

Leo leaned back.

"Damn."

Scott lit a cigarette.

Jimmy reached down for the dog.

"You done?"

"Yep."

"Can't pay for expensive education with you at the table," Leo said.

"Neither can I."

Colin smoked, wanted to keep playing.

I sat in for a few hands, won one and got out.

Colin reached over the table, scraped in another pot.

German Shorthair watched the flame as I lit a cigarette.

"Whose dog?"

"Scott's."

"She's a sweetheart."

"Why don't you put up that new bike I heard about," Scott said.

I made a revolted face.

"That's a shame," Leo reckoned.

"What kind is it?" asked Jimmy.

I told him and everybody moaned because they fantasized it could have been won. I shook my head. Colin finally laughed out loud. He took out a joint and we got high passing it around. The little cherry zinged and the dry leaf went pop, pop. The dog lay down beside me. I had to stretch to touch her fur.

Scott and Leo went over by the fire door and propped it open.

"Jimmy throw me that pack."

They smoked standing half outside.

"Was a little stuffy," Leo said.

I joined them by the door, looked up, inhaled the clean air. Leo breathed a white cloud into the dark. Dog stood up, thought she might be going out. Went over to Jimmy.

"I'm going to check upstairs," I said.

Jimmy also looked interested in going up. Thinking about it. He'd been losing badly. Didn't know what he was doing. Other two at least knew, stubborn. Jimmy took it well. Really only played for fun like me.

"I could go," he said.

Think he was glad somebody came up with an out for him.

Colin, who had never left the table, hoping there was more to come.

"I think we'll stay, see if we can get something back," said Scott.

Tossed his cigarette, he and Leo returned to the table.

Watched the two square off with Colin.

"Catch you later," he said.

Dog looking at Jimmy and I.

Jimmy and I went out the fire door into the air, were in the back looking up a hill, long flight of concrete steps. Stairs ragged, crumbling in places leading all the way up behind the old carriage house. Tried to go quickly but the height of each step much less than our natural stride so we bumped along without any light holding on to the pipe rail.

The climb winded us. Jimmy bent over examining his right knee. Went around front following a footpath emerging in the parking area.

Trees towered wherever we were. Voices at a hum mixed with music. Floodlights by the house. Girls talking, guys thinking how they could break in. Clouds around a moon, no where else in the sky. Around the clouds at their edge was a bright halo, perfect blurry circle and fantastic pale yellow.

Old music helped the girls.

Jimmy and I, speaking not long to some we saw beneath the trees. He of course knew most everyone while I followed. I was told to stop talking to a certain girl because she was an easy time. I didn't care but it vexed me their disapproval.

"We'll go inside," he said.

Past the door I stood at the rail above the great room. Jimmy went for the stairs off to the right. It was a building that seemed as if overwrought. Heard Jimmy yell from below when he realized I wasn't behind him.

Bar was in a nook behind the great room, up two steps from the main floor.

People there but in conversation deep.

The drink tasted faintly sweet as the ice reassuringly banged around inside the glass.

Sat at the bar not speaking of anything as controversial. One guy in particular felt strongly. His friends listened then responded just as resoundingly.

"What are you doing?"
Knew the voice.
"Wondered if I'd see you."
Leigh.
"Did you know I was here?"

"I saw you."

"You did?"

"Glad you came," she said.

"Can you stay?"

Centered a stool for her.

"You're still with Anson?"

"Yes."

"What about the summer?"

"I'll still be with him."

"What are you doing this summer?"

"Oh. Working."

"Good."

"What about you?"

"Working too."

I think she thought I was non-committal.

Jimmy finished his drink.

"We're going up soon," I said.

Leigh looked at me.

"Can you go?"

"I want to go."

"Need to ask?" I said.

She scoffed.

The three of us went up the stairs to the foyer. I held the door open for them.

Took Leigh to a dark quiet place. Hoped we wouldn't see Anson.

It was probably the last big night before everyone left. We watched all the antics.

She and I walked down the drive beneath the reaching trees. I heard tuned engines revving. Two riders were going to drag. Crowd gathered. Leigh and I were right in front. Six hundred pound bees and the noise thrummed our insides.

Two motorcycles shot down the lane. Close race, sure one of the riders was going to crash. I thought he had to be drunk.

Leigh had taken her hand away from her mouth, looked at me deeply.

"They made it," she said.

We went toward the house.

Introduced Colin and Leigh.

"How much did you make tonight?"

"One-seventy-five."

"That helps."

He kept looking at her.

He told us more about the game, surprised she was actually interested.

"Joss, I'm going to sit on the sofa over there."

"Tired?"

"Just wanna sit."

Maybe the smoke I thought.

Looked over at Leigh sometimes. She slipped out of the room. Last time I saw she was talking with a friend.

Book III

Jimmy found Colin and I a room. In the morning we had breakfast in the dining hall. Once again the pleasantness of the morning ritual supplanted an otherwise bleary waking.

We ate hot homemade food while most everyone else slept. When I was finished went back to the room for a couple things I accidentally left. Creaked up the warped stairs to the third floor where it was still quiet and dim. Found my wallet, leaving I saw Anson in the hall wearing a towel.

"Good morning."

"Did you have a good night?"

We creaked toward each other in the poor light.

"Yeah."

"You're always welcome."

"Thank you."

"Why don't you think about staying with us next year?"

"I could."

"Why don't you?"

"If you change your mind."

He went into the bath.

No matter what I preferred being on my own. Anson once told me I might be too freethinking. Could be too different for my own good.

Colin in the rear of the dining hall looking out a window. I went over. Behind us was the clinking of silverware and glasses as some others ate. Heard the cook's unmistakable laugh from the kitchen. Hoped Jimmy would appear but didn't get to see him.

Said hello to a few early risers as we made our way to the door. Floor in the foyer and other common areas already being scrubbed. The smell of the cleaner made me remember many things. We left by the stately entrance before an enclave where an urn filled part way with sand used as an ashtray was brimming over. Gloomy outside where it was raining, rather misting. Walked down the drive, Colin lit a cigarette.

Went along tight one way streets and neighborhood alleys under white and gray sky. Usually splitting the road till a car came.

"Who was she last night?"
"I know her."
"What happened?"
"What?"
"Something happen?"
"No."
"She likes you."
"Likes to see me sometimes."
The drizzle stopped.
"More than that," he said.

There weren't many people out. We took our time and looked in shop windows. I believe to rest. We mentioned how full we were and how tired. There was a man on a ladder scraping paint from the front of one of the buildings. He said he wanted to get it done before it got too hot. The paint was chalky red and he was going to be there for a while. Colin warned me to step around the ladder.

The bike had been knocked over. Lay on its side near the wall in the breezeway. Stomach instantly did a flip. Wondered who could have done it. Didn't seem new anymore as it lay there on its face. It was a flattening sight. Also wondered how long it had been like that. Too heavy for most people, righting it would be a strain. I tried to right a heavy American made machine before alone and something inside me popped.

Colin was disgusted too. Bent over with me to see any damage. I couldn't tell with it rolled over. We raised the bike, stood looking at it. Were some things wrong. Landed solidly on the concrete, gotten banged up.

"Who do you think?"

Shook my head.

Could have been anyone. It had to have been someone because it wouldn't fall by itself. Could have if the kickstand were over soil but not concrete. Made no sense to think it would fall over where it was. My mind couldn't stop expanding because she was raped and covered with cuts.

"There's not too much damage," he said.

I tried to calm down.

It was just the daring.

I looked closely at everything, it needed only minor work.

"You're in luck, right?"

He started going up.

Bike was upright but in the open. Would be for a few more days. I went up trying to forget everything for a while.

"You should call the police."

"Call the police and report it."

I had no desire then for the police.

I didn't do much throughout the day. Sleep or read off and on. Slept when my mind wouldn't let go of the same idea, kept repeating. I was only over rested. I went into the living room to look from the window mostly out of habit. House seemed empty. I poured a soft drink over ice, heard the bubbles, cracking sound. Looking to the west at the twilight. The apartment was quiet and still.

Before light faded I wanted to go downstairs and have another look. Thoughts were nagging me. Small scars in the fiberglass. Those bothered me most because they were harder to repair. The bent taillight, foot pedal, brake lever, fairly easy.

I was past dwelling on who it may have been. Maybe only someone passing by being destructive on a whim. I ran the motor, listening close, like I knew something would be wrong, nothing, raw vrrooom! That sounded fine. I rode out of the lot just to be sure, took it on the open road. After a short ride was convinced nothing else had been upset.

He sat near the open glass door smoking, talking on the phone. Waved as I came in. No time to exhale, smoke running from his nose and mouth.

"Diana," he said.

"Haven't seen her for a while."

"You'll see her tomorrow."

I nodded, unsure.

"Parents will be here. We'll pack, find somewhere to eat."

"Make sure you're around."

"I'll leave a note telling you the place."

"Any plans tonight?" I asked.

"On my own."

I didn't want to ride, wanted to walk.

"After they leave tomorrow night I'm wide open. Plan to spend as much time as I can with Diana."

"When are you finished?"

"Friday."

"What about taking a trip up?" he asked.

"Yeah, I'd like to go."

"Great to see the water. Have a place for the weekend."

He was excited.

"People I'd like you to meet while you're up."

The meal was served and as we ate we talked about some of the things that had happened. We wondered about the future and what to look out for. All of it needed to be said, turned over, examined, validated and justified. Volumes of dreams, thoughts and ideas, once aired out, surely would come true. As we spoke felt like we were doing them, doing something about it, made it real, wouldn't have to worry about falling on our faces or missing out. It was great to let someone like him know that I would not fall on my face.

We were no longer in our surroundings, the walls fell away. Alone on a new plane. All the questions, concerns and apprehension reasoned away, only for those who would accept any limitations.

We ran out of words, our mouths were dry. We made blank expressions; I felt the cold glass in my hand.

Fresh breeze, scenery unstuck a tired view.
   "Believe that all can happen?"
   He put his face in the wind.
   We walked amid fantastic gardens.
   He seemed looking for understanding.
   I was always happy with only a clear conscience.

I got an early start Sunday keeping in mind I would need to be free later to meet his parents. Once in a while I got working early. Even food tasted better, I almost believed.

Time dripped away. I shifted constantly in my chair made of flat wood to keep it from wearing through to my tailbone. The slightest movement from others seemed a touch rude from the corners of my eyes and in the forced quiet my mind started to get eaten away before the task.

Energy was scarce having woken so early. By the time I was walking out of the library I was ready to relax. Colin and his parents and Diana were in the living room all drinking something and laughing quietly when I arrived. His folks were using the best cheap glasses in our store.

"There he is!" Colin announced.

I was introduced to his mother and father then spoke with Diana briefly while the other three tried to decide where we should eat.

Colin did not look like either of his parents. Possibly the eyes. His mother and father possessed a certain intensity. Whatever they had, believed they worked hard for.

"Joss, do you have a preference?" his mother asked me.

"There's a place you might like."

"What's it called?"

"Hardway's."

"Forgot that place."

"Not a good sign," his father said.

"Out of our range."

"I see."

"Let's go," Colin said.

Everyone agreed, Diana smiled at me.

We all met at the door.

His dad drove a big car. Understood he had some kind of mold making business. He bought the company when he was fed up with being an actuary. I thought being an actuary sounded interesting. Maybe it was only the word itself that was.

"Did you get everything?" I asked.

"Almost everything's in the trunk," his father answered.

I liked his dad. He liked driving his big car. He leaned back casually and had his hand draped over the wheel steering with his wrist and thumb. The car was dark blue, favorite of mine. Upholstery on the seats was a kind of plush fabric. I rubbed my fingers on it to see it change hue. Colin's mom

smoked close to the window open a crack. Diana was between Colin and I in back, hands on her knees.

"You didn't have that much did you Col?"

"Nope. Only clothes and other small stuff. Rest was there
when I came."

His father nodded, looked at us in the rearview. I could
only see his mother's abundant brown hair by the window.
She seemed interested in what we passed by.

"Are you hungry, Mrs. Wight?" Diana asked.

Colin's mother cleared her throat, threw out the cigarette.
"Mm-hmm."

Colin squeezed Diana's hand.

We listened to his father tell stories about his business and
other feats while we ate. The family was bored hearing it but
I enjoyed images of the world outside. Thought it was good
to envision what lie ahead. But like so many who tell stories,
they tend to repeat. I had a feeling they had heard those
things before. He wasn't repeating anything to me. I even
asked questions. Soon it was just his dad and myself. The
others were off on something else. Colin's mom finally
spoke freely. Diana relaxed since his mom relaxed.

No one was drinking at our pace.

Colin and I were the only ones having vodka.

It was an evil slush with the ice.

"You're both going to enjoy being away for a while."

"We need a break badly, mom."

"I know you do, honey."

His mother missed the joke.

I felt slightly guilty.

Colin made a big grin.

His father laughed heartily and the table brightened another notch.

"Nice place, Joss, thanks for the suggestion," his father mentioned.

Diana and I trailed behind Colin and his parents.

"What are you two doing?" she asked.

We drove home and the four of them shuttled a few more things down to the car when we got there. I thanked his mom and dad, left he and Diana alone with them.

I got up before the sun again. Maybe the birds are meant to make you feel like you are not the only one. I went out on the ledge and had a breakfast of overdone toast then got dressed after quickly bathing. I had just a little time so I began to read at the front table. When I was done I packed up everything and went into my room.

I knew after taking the first exam I had been fairly prepared and was doing something right. I came to realize I needed to learn how to take tests. Finished that first one, felt as if I passed but refused to think about it much because I couldn't spare any concern.

I hadn't ridden the last few days and delighted in the sound of the engine warming. That primitive music kept satisfying. I rode out and had to be the first customer at Big Mike's shop that morning. The sun was barely high enough above the trees and other buildings to show through the glass onto the rows of inventory. I leaned on the counter in back until a man with overalls and a t-shirt under approached me from the garage.

"Help you?"

I explained what happened and asked him if he could write up a repair estimate. He went in back again and came out with a clipboard. He stepped from behind the counter, inquisitively grunted, saw the motorcycle, and went that way. He put his hands on his hips and looked at the bike then knelt down for a closer look. He looked intently at some things then would write something down, shuffle along, still squatting, looking for something else. I said a few words that I thought might help but he only nodded to be polite because he knew he would see it on his own.

"Not too bad, huh?"

He shook his head, his face told me.

He went back inside, over to the counter.

He looked in some guide.

"We'll need to keep it a couple days."

"This much?"

Just his empty expression.

The insurance office was a comfortless place that needed freshening. The awning above the front door seemed to look worse on brighter days that revealed how much color it had lost, mostly faded out with a solid hint of the original shade near a rib. Cramped standing there with those two again. I was sure nothing about them had changed and it appeared they hadn't moved either. Air was hovering a light gray between the block walls that would lean visibly closer.

♦

The pair looked up at me from their efficient chairs behind the counter.

"May we help you?" the man asked.

I ignored his pretension, began to explain what happened. He seemed almost irritated. So I just described it broadly.

"What do you have there?"

I watched him lighten as he read the numbers, freehand on dealer letterhead.

"Did you notify the police?"

The question hung.

"Did they give you something?"

Never called the police.

"What happened?"

"It was vandalized."

"Someone knocked it over."

I knew better than to supply details. He handed the sheet to the woman. Examined the form, man pointed at a couple items. She began to type. He made himself busy behind the counter, allowed a genuine expression once, noticed me accidentally. She now stopped. More conferring, clacked on. She knew how to work the conjuring machine. Bell sounded, zinged the carriage over to start another line. Turned the roller, grabbed out my check.

"Just need you to sign here and here," he said.

I leaned over, signed where he asked, folded the check away.

Both looked more meaningful.

I left the bike at the dealership for them to fit into their schedule.

"We'll call you," overalls told me.

"How long?"

"Probly Thursday."

Filled out the work ticket, gave him the keys, used a phone.

Wanted to ride back in a taxicab, obvious sedan was soon in front.

Air ran in the window I rolled down.

Colin was seated at the table eating lunch, captured by whatever he was reading.

"Took the bike in to get worked on."

"Good."

"Uh huh."

"When did they tell you it would be ready?"

"Thursday."

He nodded.

"Should be ready by then."

"Say anything else?"

"Not much to it."

"You ever find out who did it?"

"No. Got money for the damage."

"Yeah?"

"Guess that's it."

He shrugged.

"We have no idea?"

"Well."

"What should I do, hunt em down?"

That sounded okay.

He laughed.

"You surprise me," he said.

"Howzat?"

"I don't know."

"We'll see."

♦

Most of the time thereafter for me was spent in seclusion. Literally hid myself away preparing for exams. Never easy, could make me act somewhat odd. Self-imposed, anti-social behavior that temporarily cut ties with fellow human beings for such a purpose always left me ragged.

The week so far had been bad, when my father and step-mother arrived that morning felt I was close to exhaustion. I hadn't seen either of them since the holidays last winter. Old feelings of dread came over me. We exchanged nervous greetings then I said something that was really nothing, set her off, things were right back the way they were. She could facilitate such anxiety. How she enjoyed pushing people around. How I wished she would simply vanish away. I tried ignoring her, I just needed to give them my things to take back.

At last we were packing, hauling things to the car without saying much. Any conversation was strained, controlled, otherwise bad silence. Some can't get past what they are, can't see. I have never been so convinced of myself I could not change.

"Is there anything else?" Dad asked.

"Think you have it all."

"When will we be seeing you?"

"Maybe Sunday."

"Okay, take care, son. We'll look forward to Sunday."

The words sounded forced but I think he meant it. He embraced me by the car. Stepmother waved with her back to me as she slid into the passenger seat. All the religion in the world didn't seem to work.

"See you."

My dad smiled sadly, opened his door.

I watched them go.

He waved to me before going around the turn.

I saw Carrie in the breezeway sweeping the entrance of her apartment.

"Parents?"

"Yeah."

"Visiting?"

"Pick up."

"I'm going too."

"Home?"

"Later today."

"Where?"

"Greensburg."

She didn't think I'd heard of it. She looked great there in the breezeway. Knelt down, swept the dirty pile into the dustpan.

They took all my things except what I thought I would need over the next few days. Some clothes are all I had. Bobby was gone already, maybe to start work. I don't remember him leaving. I honestly don't remember seeing him go. Our ritual aloofness must have driven him off. The bedroom felt sterile, sound bounced between six open planes.

I didn't want to hide away another night in the belly of some awful library. I looked ahead to some rest and the weekend. Getting to it was uphill and seemed far off. Colin missed my father and stepmother. Made himself scarce. He understood. I resented the whole damn thing. Wished people could have restrained themselves. What a mess that I could not seem to fix.

♠

It was late and he was asleep on the carpet in front of the slider. I wanted something to eat and hung in front of the fridge with the door open.

I think he'd been drinking by himself. Eventually got to his feet, turned on the radio. I almost cried because I was so exhausted, too weak for another emotion.

The next day it was over. The highwaymen who held me up for my books marked the finality. What little money they gave was almost worth not having to haul the obsolete manuals around.

"How did it go?"

"Glad I'm through."

His anticipation helped with my revival.

"Hi Joss."

"Hi Diana."

She walked into the room tucking in her shirt, tank on the back of the commode refilling.

"You helping Colin pack?"

"I'll bring whatever he can't take next week."

"That'll be most of it."

They looked at each other, already had that conversation.

"I think it's ready," Colin said.

Diana raised her eyebrows evocatively.

"They were supposed to call yesterday."

Colin placed his bag by the door.

"Going out for a late breakfast, take you on the way."

"Okay."

"I just want to finish everything here," he said.

I put on my boots and changed my shirt.

He hauled up his bag and I came from behind, opened the door. We spoke at once excitedly down the stairs. Colin opened the trunk of Diana's car to put in the duffel then got behind the wheel. He wasn't able to take much the way we were going so she would have to bring the extra. He couldn't really take anything with him but the clothes he was wearing. He'd have whatever he would need once we got there.

We were driving the bridge to downtown. I was beginning to feel all right, no thanks to the head jarring pressure. The sun was shining, few clouds. Muddy water still nice and deep running below.

"Meet you back in an hour!"

The mechanic who did the work wasn't there but another man helped me. He showed me the bike, said it was finished and ready to go. It looked like new, amazed at how they did it, especially some of the jagged scratches toward the front.

He saw I was pleased and went to the counter to find the bill.

"Any problems?"

He shrugged saying no quietly.

I paid with cash and he handed me the keys with a paper tag.

I took some of the cash to fill the tank. I didn't know if one tank was going to be enough. Thought it might be close. There was a man selling sandwiches on the corner, ate something while I sat on the bike next to the curb. I had black fingers the aroma of fuel.

The apartment was empty, few pieces of furniture nobody wanted. Some of Mark's things were there. I put my clothes in a light pack. Watched by the glass door waiting for Colin.

"You ready?"

Diana was holding onto him.

"Yep."

"Let's get going."

Diana was acting nervous.

"Wish I was going too."

"I'll see you soon," Colin assured her.

She made a childlike face, hugged him.

"I have to go to work!"

Tears were welling up in her eyes.

"Take care Joss. I'll miss you."

She hugged me.

I didn't have the words.

"Maybe I'll see you," she said.

She gave Colin another hug.

"Look out for each other."

Diana stood by the door with her arms crossed. Then she was out of sight, heard her footsteps echoing down the stairs.

Slung the pack over my shoulder.

The contented spacecat in his sunglasses.

I put mine on soon too.

I sent the helmet back, packed it carefully so it would not be found.

We went out.

He followed locking the door.

I handed him the pack at the bike. If I wore it on my back he would have been pushed off the seat.

We made a stop at the rental office to drop off keys.

Weather could not have been better. We would ride under big sky. He lit a cigarette at a stop sign before we started along the river to the highway.

We bumped over groups of tracks, passed an isolated depot where the commuter train stopped. Area I thought would be lively.

Two and a half hours riding, landscape changed dramatically. No longer flat. Beige dunes rose up beside the access roads leading to the curved tip of the lake, its southernmost point.

His spirit transformed.

"This way."

He pointed as we undid the tangle of roads cut around sandy mountains, increasing stands of trees.

Slopes were gradual, rolling, sudden and high. Pavement struggling to keep up. Going carefully around turns, avoid feathers of sand left by the wind.

Turning uphill reached a clear spot, he asked to pull over. Looked across the cold blue lake, billowy wonders towering up like steam. Day was clear and deep blue went on and on. Could see faint white lines from boats cutting the water as many haphazard scratches.

Downside faster going, glided and braked. Surrounded by evergreen trees. Air cooler around back, smelled of pine and moisture.

Getting ready to go around the curve.

"Here!"

I started to roll up the drive. Engine off could hear the waves faintly. Ranch style home poised in the trees above the lake.

He handed over the pack. Opened the garage so I could put the bike in. I followed him up the stepped walk to the front door. There was a note taped to the glass which he removed.

He easily found the key.

Above more steps in the entry could see straight to the back of the house. My gaze was instantly drawn to the picture window.

"Make yourself at home."

Shadowy almost dark. Went over and put a knee on the sofa in front of the north facing window. Behind the glass Lake Michigan more like a painting than real. Deepest blue, painter had also been able to capture how cold it must be.

I turned and he passed in front of me to the kitchen.

"Where are your parents?"

"Be back later."

"You told them I was coming?"

"Yes, you'll be in the spare room downstairs by mine."

I sat down but kept staring out.

"I'll find a cooler, we'll spend the day by the water."

I was shown my room.

He located the cooler.

He slid open the screen door off the kitchen with a finger then went down the sun blanched steps from the deck behind the house. After the stairs was a path in the sand and it was a new feeling touching the rustling beach grass as we walked toward the shore that rumbled ahead.

The path sloped above a sand cliff. Trail actually circled in front of the dune. We found a place to spread out near the tumbling waves.

He leaned back on his towel supporting himself with his elbows.

"Good to be home."

I floated just above the sand.

Slept off and on. Wind sliding over us.

With evening approaching the temperature began to fall. Brown sand complimented the light dimming to orange.

Colin put on a sweatshirt.

"Simon."

He stood up and gave his friend a handshake then put his arm around the other's neck. Colin could produce a smile that overtook everything.

Simon turned free from him, held out his hand.

"Nice to meet you."

"The same," he said.

Colin opened the cooler to offer Simon a beer.

"So how is it up here?" said Simon.

"Great!"

I don't think the question was for me.

Simon nodded patiently. He had dark hair cut short and was my height. Athletic. His face was friendly and he had a quietness.

"Bout you?"

"Good to be back," Colin said.

I enjoyed listening to Simon while it grew dark. Fire close by beckoned us. Colin tried to hand out one hits and asked who wanted the last beer. Colin and Simon knew most everyone and each time were greeted warmly. I sat on the cooler sipping a beer someone gave me, unconsciously drawn by the windy flame while they genially talked with all their friends.

We were offered hot food and they gave us beer from their coolers. In the middle I looked at Colin who was home and happy.

"Got to run up but I'll be back soon," he said.

"Be right here."

"We've known each other since we were little."

Simon sitting down next to me.

"Hell of a skipper, you'll probably see tomorrow."

The word made me smile.

"You didn't want to leave?"

"Had to wait."

I looked at him. Fire popped. Simon lit a cigarette, asked if I could have one.

Colin beside me again.

"What's happening up top?"

"They're home. Going to bed soon. Say hello, look forward to seeing you in the morning."

It took him some time to scrounge a beer.

The faces across lit only by the whims of the fire.

"How's Diana?" asked Simon.

"She's fine."

"Lotta girls running around up here."

I turned my head.

"Weather is supposed to be perfect in the morning. I'll be on the water early," Simon shared.

"What time?" I asked.

"How's eight?"

"I'll be down."

"See you in the morning."

"You going?"

Red coals with short flames between filled the fire pit.

"Known him for a long time."

"That's what he said."

"Did almost everything growing up."

Warmth of the fire was making me drowsy, wanted to stretch out.

We gathered our things, said goodnight to the few that were left. I followed Colin up the path. Sand cold on my feet. High stepped along the trail, pushed myself up the wooden stairs to the sliding door. The house was dark except for a candle in the center of the dining table. He cupped it with his hand and blew it out. I couldn't see a thing.

"This way."

I followed his sound to steps lit by footlights.

"Let me know if you need anything."

"Thanks."

"Yep, goodnight."

♣

I went into the room, took off my jacket, noticed everything was ready. Extra blankets and towels were on the bed. O-pened the window, heard the water rushing the sand out there in the dark. Put on a clean t-shirt to slide between the sheets.

At that hour, mist floated in the trees. Quietly dressed, made my way to the beach. Went out from downstairs. Sand still cold but the earth's surface now nice and malleable. Fog re-treated away from the shoreline going inland. Saw Simon rigging his boat at the water's edge. Girl with him also busy with the readying.

"Good morning!"

"Good morning."

"This is my sister Dandy."

"Hello."

"Go inside that box and find a vest," he said.

I did as he said, returned to the boat to see what I could do to help.

"Your job will be to keep us low in the water if the wind picks up."

"Okay."

"You ever been out on one of these?"

"Just one hull."

"These little catamarans can go a lot faster."

Freezing water around my ankles. Dandy and Simon on one side and me on the other drug the lightweight boat all the way in and had to hold onto it firmly because the waves wanted to shove it back ashore. When we were about mid thigh deep I was instructed to climb onto the canvas. Water was frigid and my legs tingled.

"You coming?" I asked.

"Just here to help," Dandy said.

She had sharp features, hair long and brown, rounded shoulders. Guessed she was younger than Simon. She held onto the boat as he joined me.

Sail flew against a northwest breeze.

"You see where the water's darker? Whitecaps?"

Had to turn to look.

I understood that's where we were headed. The water changed from clear green to navy. Line was distinct. Beyond it looked suddenly very deep. Imagined a bottom that virtually fell away. Wondered what was at the edge.

Gust of wind tightened the sail.

"Here we go."

He motioned for me to move to a place over the windward hull. I went steadily. It was the early season, wind took us, tiny boat was a knife through the waves.

Hull slapped the surface. Simon glanced at me and I knew to hold on. He held the line tight as the boat lifted then would slam down. Fly over the crest of a wave then stick in the trough.

"Whooo—hooo!"

Boat jumped, water sprayed everywhere.

"You ever sail like this before!"

Whooshing water.

We sailed to the place where the water changed. Watched the transformation. Lighter water had been friendlier. Dark only contrasted the white on the crests of the waves more. Suddenly our boat was even smaller. It seemed there was nothing below. The dark blue went on forever. The swells seemed to magnify. Simon came about and we turned away.

Shoreline appeared remote. Difficult for me to tell which section of beach we had come from. I remembered to watch for the yellow box.

A boat approached coming straight ahead. Colin. He turned his boat into the wind, switched sides to give chase. He was lighter, soon caught up. Seemed to be above us.

Simon hollered. I held on as we went up, dove into a trough, wind caught us sending us up again. Colin staggered beyond.

I was almost used to the cold water. Each boat stayed even in the shallows, dark outlines of things on the lake floor.

Simon loosened the sail, took us in. We bumped into the sand. Colin going out again. Simon and I hauled our craft farther ashore.

"What do you think?"

"Unbelievable!"

He took off his vest and dove in. Crazy.

Simon and I sat on the beach talking about the voyage. Watched Colin as he came back, sail gray and black. Helped him drag the boat.

Colin dripping wet, more than a little invigorated. Stood next to his boat, dried off. He and Simon exchanged a few words about the conditions.

"Anyone hungry, want breakfast?"

I looked at Simon, didn't see his sister.

"Why don't we go up?"

Colin's mother sat at the kitchen table holding a coffee mug. I could smell smoke but didn't believe she'd done it indoors.

"How was it this morning?" she asked.

"Fantastic!"

Simon and Colin murmured laughter.

"Good," she said.

She looked at us.

"You know your brother is coming next Saturday."

"I remember," Colin said.

"You haven't seen each other."

"But isn't he leaving again?"

"To go on his internship."
"Where?"
"Massachusetts."
Simon and I sat down at the table.
"Wanted to remind you."
"Very smart guy."
"Let me get you breakfast."
"Anything, mom."
"Eggs, waffles?"
"Can you do both?"
"Are you that hungry?"
"Okay, both."
"Where's dad?"
"Had to go in for a little bit."
She put on an apron. I found my friend's mom attractive.
Kitchen began to fill with smells. He and Simon talked about
the water.

Nothing was left over.
"That was good."
"Anytime, Simon, you know that."
"Have a job I need to finish," he said.
"Really?"
"What are you doing?"
The mother running the water.
"Started landscaping."
"Lot of work?"
"Getting there."
"Think we need our lawn mowed."
"Yeah, funny."
"What are you doing today?" Simon asked.
"Probably go back out later," Colin said.
"I'll tell Dandy."
I leaned back uncomfortably full.

"Do you want to sail this afternoon?" Colin asked me.

"Yeah."

"Mind if I went out for a while?"

"Nope."

"You'll be okay?"

"Of course."

"Won't be gone long."

We thanked his mother again, went downstairs.

"Be back in a while."

He'd gotten dressed. Heard the outside door swat shut. I leaned on the windowsill; watched boats on the boiling dark go back and forth. Some I noticed only because they reflected sunlight.

Rested on the bed for a few minutes then took a shower. Put on a pair of shorts and the same shirt, followed the path to shore. Few sunbathers dotted the beach in either direction. Spread my towel.

Sun didn't seem it would burn till I lay facing it, wanted to swim but wasn't ready for ice from fire.

Walked to the water, surge around my ankles, hint of it was enough. But waded in to my thighs, big shiver.

Shadow of a cloud landed on me.

"Thinking about a job?"

"Not today."

Colin sat down smoking a cigarette.

Wondered if he bought pot, saw a girlfriend. Said he just went for a look around, picked up some cigs.

"Peaceful here," he said.

"You mean am I enjoying myself?"

I sat up Indian style. Reached for the cigarettes.

"I won't be going back in the fall," he told me.

"I know."

He leaned on his hands.

"What are you going to do?"

"Not sure."

He glanced at me then to the water.

I knew I couldn't talk to him.

There was a girl walking alone coming toward us. First she looked as if she might pass by then we realized it was Dandy.

"Little girl," he called.

Dandy stood in front of us.

"You found us," I said.

"Simon told me."

"You want to sail?" asked Colin.

"Just wanted to come down."

Dandy sat. She had on a peach one piece with a towel wrapped around her waist.

"When are you going out?"

"Now," he said.

He grinned at her like he was going to eat her.

She laughed, smiled unbelievably. He'd known her a long time too.

He and I pulled the boat up to the water. Dandy waded in raising her towel. She also had a quietness made her seem strong. She must be loved very much I thought. I put on a vest, Colin inspected the rudder.

The boat was set, three of us drug her in.

"You going?" Colin asked.

"You go, it's a nice wind," she said.

"You can come,"

"It's all right."

"Okay, jump on!" he told me.

Dandy helped steady. Lake was rough so we had to climb onto the canvas deeper in.

"Big waves," he said lifting his chin.

"If we go over, push away."

"I will."

"Ready?"

Colin drew in the line slowly, filling up the sail. Decided I was going to stay back from the edge as long as possible. The small boat jetted forward and we bounced over the waves, sometimes flying from the top of one to the top of another. All around was steel blue and the huge water looked ominous as it rolled and shifted wildly.

Both of us gradually leaned out trying to keep her down as we picked up speed. At ease in the chaos. We crashed violently into the lumbering swells, sometimes putting the bow under, drenching us with all the spray. He would then loosen the sail to bring us smoothly out of the trough. Figures on the beach became too small to recognize.

Jarring impact, Colin let out the wind, attempted to come about. Lake was thunderous beyond that point.

"This is going to happen fast, watch your head!"

He waited for what he thought was just the right time.

"Here we go!"

Followed him under the boom which swung over in an instant. We had been too far into the wind. When it hit the fabric it forced us over, capsized. I was flying. Saw Colin go in while I continued on beyond. Flash behind my eyes from the splitting cold.

"You okay!"

"I'm all right!"

We were in the black water.

"I'm going to need your help! Just do what I do!"

He swam around to climb up on the lower hull side.

"Come up here with me."

I swam over, climbed onto the hull side's slick surface. Sail wasn't deep under yet. Standing on the end of the lower hull and grabbing hold of the end of the other he began leaning back and pulling. Saw what he was trying to do, leaned back and rocked with him.

"Use you legs. When it starts to roll, hold on as long as you can then get away."

We leaned back pulling hard against the hull. Mast began to rise out of the water. The boat came toward us and was going to go. We pushed out to keep from getting our heads cracked.

The sail flapped in the wind. We climbed up.

"What happened?"

He laughed a bit disgustedly.

We had to come about, conditions that moment were better, he'd eased the sail.

Sailed more gracefully thereafter. Seagulls flew above us and I watched the sunlight held by the water.

We glided up to shore clear of the break.

Dandy had her vest on. Colin patiently went out with her. It was his boat she said so he had to go. But she wanted captain. They didn't go as far out but farther along the shore.

They were out of view so I went to lying on the sand. Clean, polished feeling after the water.

Their voices carried, I sat up. Dandy still at the helm, Colin sitting comfortably on the canvas as they pointed in.

She and Colin squared the boat away.

"Why don't we cook down here tonight?" he said.

Dandy wanted to.

"Sure there's meat at the house."

Colin went up to see about food. Had to put my shirt on to keep from getting too burned. Back and shoulders were getting red.

I told her about the motorcycle, she wanted to see it so we made our way to the garage.

Mr. Wight was there studying the lawn. He said Colin drove off somewhere. Dandy looked at the bike but couldn't appreciate it fully. She borrowed a shirt and sandals from

Colin's mother and we went for a ride. The roads were too twisted, wondered how much she liked it.

Colin was still not back. Dandy said she was going home and would meet us later. I talked with Colin's father then went inside and made something to drink. Colin's mother actually made it, brought it to me on the deck. She said Colin went to buy food. The meat she had was frozen. She stayed, smoked a cigarette, went in. I sat alone with a cold pitcher. I thought about the road and going back. Not yet. Heard voices of people down below.

"Where's Joss?"

"Out there," I heard his mother say.

He came onto the deck to show me the steaks.

"Why not?" he said.

Appreciated the trouble he went to.

Colin's dad told us there was a section of grill behind the box onshore. Find wood all over.

"What else did you get?"

"Corn."

Created a blaze using pieces of dry wood that littered the beach. Found the section of grill, knocked the sand loose. I put the rack against the fire to burn away any residue. Colin smoked watching the fire. He'd bought beer, liquor. Fire soon be ready. Waiting for it to burn down. Children began to turn up, released after the family meal. Some of them came near the fire. They'd look at us then at the fire. Running back and forth trying to poke it with sticks. Whispered, chanted monotone jabs. They wanted to cook marshmallows. We said okay so they went up to get the bag.

Simon appeared with Dandy. Colin adjusted the grill over the coals. He soon put on the steaks. Corn went on too in the husk but there was protesting.

Colin squinting into the fire, turning the meat. Simon and Dandy tried rum, Simon switched to beer. Dandy liked the rum, surprising us. She was wearing a lightweight jacket and had her arms wrapped around her knees.

Kids came back around, ate black marshmallows roasted on the ends of their bent sticks, burst into laughter when they tasted the sweetness.

Everybody was surprised how good the corn was.

Colin threw me a cigarette.

Talked about sailing. Got to hear a few good stories from over the years. Dandy went for a little more rum. Her face looked precious in the light. Simon and Colin wondered if they could make a living in a beach town somewhere giving lessons and competing. I thought it would be great. Dandy hugged her knees. Colin asked her what she thought. She only laughed at him. He told her Mexico or Hawaii.

"Why there?"

He shrugged.

"Try harder."

"Against Hawaiian guys?"

Dandy shook her head.

Simon laughed into the fire.

The children had departed.

We went up to the water.

Dandy wrapped in a big towel. Just watching us, cold.

Back to the dying fire. Dandy moved in closer to the heat, sleepy. Colin and I started gathering what we brought. Moon beginning its ascent. Still a little something to drink.

Said goodnight to each other, Simon swept sand over the coals. Colin and I slowly made our way up the path to the house. Beach grass waved back and forth in the driest note.

The first thing you hear is the water. You tried to dream the water.

I lay snug under the covers.

No mist in the morning.

Silver sky.

I ate and poured the juice Mrs. Wight mixed. She was in her robe; I was still wearing what I slept in. She'd glance at my hair occasionally.

She and I talked at the table. Told me I was welcome to stay.

I went onto the deck into the silky air and watched boats.

Colin still was not up, wanted to try and catch Simon only a few houses down.

After saying goodbye to him I went to the beach.

"Good walk?"

Colin was rinsing dishes in the sink when I came in.

"You like it here," he said.

"Yeah."

"You leaving soon?"

"Clean up downstairs first."

"Don't worry about that."

"My stuff."

"Take your time."

I straightened the towels, made the bed. Stood in the window for a moment watching Colin as he talked to a neighbor outside. He was energized.

I put the things I brought into the pack, went to the garage. One of the cars was gone. Hung the pack over the bike's handlebars, went around the side of the house.

Went down to the beach where he was sitting on his boat.
It almost helped quietly talking.
He explained what some of the floating markers meant.
Might get down this summer he thought.
Good just to sit with him.
Hard walk up the hill.
The big door opened behind me.
I rolled the bike out and he stepped back when the engine started.
"You can wear that now!"
He meant the pack.
I gripped his hand and we quick looked at each other.
Now clicked the lever.
Turned in the seat and waved to Colin who kept standing there.

To receive additional copies of this book or to send a gift please visit www.cadanhenry.com or use the form below:

Burden Books, PO Box 501938, Indianapolis, IN 46250

Please send me _____ copy(s) of Cadan Henry's *Cigarettes Around the Room*. I am enclosing $14.95 plus $3.50 to cover postage and handling each.

Mr/Mrs/Ms_____

Address_____

City_____

State_____ Zip_____

Gift to:

Mr/Mrs/Ms_____

Address_____

City_____

State_____Zip_____

*Please allow 1-2 weeks for delivery.